WIGGLING WISHBONE

{stories of pata-sexual speculation}

NEW AUTONOMY SERIES

Jim Fleming & Peter Lamborn Wilson, Editors

TAZ
The Temporary Autonomous Zone,
Ontological Anarchy, Poetic Terrorism
Hakim Bey

This Is Your Final Warning!
Thom Metzger

Friendly Fire
Bob Black

Caliban and the Witches
Silvia Federici

First and Last Emperors
The Absolute State & The Body of the Despot
Kenneth Dean & Brian Massumi

Warcraft
Jonathan Leake

Crimes of Culture
Richard Kostelanetz

The Electronic Disturbance
Critical Arts Ensemble

This World We Must Leave
& Other Essays
Jacques Camatte

Spectacular Times
Larry Law

Future Primitive & Other Essays
John Zerzan

Whore Carnival
Shannon Bell

X-Texts
Derek Pell

Cracking the Movement
Squatting Beyond the Media
Foundation for the Advancement
of Illegal Knowledge

The Lizard Club
Steve Abbott

Invisible Governance
The Art of African Micropolitics
David Hecht & Maliqalim Simone

Wiggling Wishbone
Bart Plantenga

Pirate Utopias
Moorish Corsairs & European Renegados
Peter Lamborn Wilson

WIGGLING WISHBONE

{stories of pata-sexual speculation}

"Pataphysics is the science of imaginary solutions...
& will describe a universe which can be—&
perhaps should be—envisaged in the
place of the traditional one..."
▸ Alfred Jarry

bart plantenga

Autonomedia

Autonomedia
po box 568 brooklyn, ny 11211-0568

phone & fax: 718-963-2603

The author was born in Amsterdam & spent his formative years in toxic Central Jersey. He's the author of 4.5 novels—including *Confessions of a Beer Mystic (a novel of beer & light)* & *Womanizer*—and is DJ of "WReCk ThiS meSS" at Radio Libertaire in Paris & WFMU in NY-NJ.

He can be contacted directly at
219 dean street
brooklyn ny 11217

printed in the United States of America

WIGGLING CONTENTS

introduction(s)

artwork(s)

WISHBONE INTERDICTION

I'm gonna move into your neighborhood, make
the value of your property go down.
• Bo Diddley

Some of these stories have appeared in other forms in the following: *Lowest Common Denominator, Screw, Big Fish, Joe Soap's Canoe, Massacre, Murtaugh, National Poetry Magazine of the Lower Eastside, Aquarian Weekly, Sensitive Skin, Beet, Rant, Wray* & others.

Some were performed at the following: Biblios, Cedar Tavern, Max Fish, CB's Gallery, Ave. B Garden, Gas Station, No Bar, Nuyorican Poets Cafe, Eureka Joe's, Fez Under Time Cafe, Pyramid, Right Bank, Anseo, Stanton Bunker, WFMU (NYC), American University, Finnegans Wake, EPE, American Church, Radio Libertaire (Paris), DAI (Heidelberg), & Globe Book Store (Prague).

The germ for the twist in vision came during the Vietnam war when I read of U.S. soldiers who proudly wore necklaces strung with the assholes of dead Viet Cong.

Mucho danken remerciments: My parents, Foto Sifichi, Shalom, Nina Ascoly, Dave Mandl, Chris Potash, Ron Kolm, Mike Golden, Maguy Berry, Yossarian, Roma Napoli, Kristin Armstrong, Sharon Mesmer, Deborah Pintonelli, La Famille Berry, Su Byron, Michael Carter, Bikini Girl, Jim Feast, Matty Jankowski, Phantom & Phantomess, Brad Weiss, Peter Lamborn Wilson, Jordan Zinovich, Jim Fleming, Gail Offen, Francesca Palazzola, Karin DeBoer, Pawel Tulin, Joe Maynard & the Unbearable Beatniks of Light, Orange, the participating artists & J. G. Ballard all who have offered their conspiratorial inspiration &/or have tolerated me as the ultimate test in benevolence.

GLOWING ART-BIOS

...for the illumination of the real by the wonderful.
• Moorish Orthodox Radio Crusade

David Sandlin: his vision of an erotic transcendent world where drunkenness & godliness converge is so uncannily close to my own vision that I'd entrust to him the docu-drama visualization of my brain on the back of my eyelids in an instant.

Shalom: adamant purveyor of post-Tinguely maximal-engagement sculpture & sinister post-Grosz portraits of our psycho-malaise. A pernicious talent from Czechoslovakia & Stanton Street.

Yossarian: former art director & contributor of his own deSade-goes-Borscht-Belt sensibility to alternative rags like *East Village Other, Screw, High Times, Ace* & *Yipster Times* from Levittown.

Dix10: J.J. Dow Jones & Roma Napoli are the legendary Parisian art partnership known for clever, ribald & acerbic takes on consumer society, conceptual plenitude & withering values.

Black Sifichi: my kinetic co-conspirator in Paris par avion. Man Ray with a 3rd eye sipping a Molotov. A true jazz butcher & photographer nonpareil.

Valerie Haller: co-caretaker of Coney Island's Sideshows by the Seashore & a tenacious artist situated somewhere between Stuart Davis & the anonymous artisans of carnival posters.

Mag Bee: unconscious talents make her incisive Matisse-limber figures seem so simple & unencumbered by human rancor. Parisian fashion designer with secrets to a floatatious lifestyle.

Kaz: fantastic psychoscapes peopled with unrequited mutants & beauties damaged by their own sinister souls. Frequenter of many speculative-gonzo zines including *Heavy Metal, Raw, LCD.*

Orange: an in-demand, meticulous & precise illustrator of many children's books.

Miss Bullard: a club-hopping folk-primitivist who specializes in dead Elvis, Pope & Peggy Lee docu-expressionism. She has never allowed life to compromise her right to fun.

Ned Sonntag: did Betty Boop, worked for Marvel, *Howard The Duck, Outlaw Biker, Young Lust & Juggs*. Wants to be known as the "Vargas of the fat glamour movement" for his loving renditions of women of Botero rotundity.

Jonathon Rosen: if Bosch had been born in cyberspace with a prosthetic drawing hand.

David Borchart: illustrator, clerical worker & Elvis impersonator. The Elvis he impersonates is from an alternate universe where Elvis was thin, introspective & unable to sing.

WOMANIZER:

A NOVEL OF EVERYDAY PARTICIPATION

Ned Sonntag

I'm a buysexual.
• **Al Goldstein, *Screw***

This new work by renowned so-called author, bart plantenga, is currently offering a unique opportunity to enter the well-furnished scenery of an actual New York novel.

Yes, for a limited time only you can become an actual participant in a steamy novel full of intrigue, passion and tragedy! Set in the splendid decay of post-fortunate Loisaida. You, as a character, will affect the action, the plot, the pants & consciousness of the main characters.

Frequent the bars, clubs, poetry readings & ambi-sexual soirees. Schmooze with scenemakers & scenetakers. Find yourself in bed, in trouble, in situations of intrigue with fascinating characters based on actual living downtown legends!

That's right, for only a small fee you can become immortalized right in the comfort of your own living room. Did you ever imagine immortality would be so easy? & fast!? (Guaranteed response time: 14 days.) Did you ever imagine that for as few as 250 of your own words describing your desires & machinations you could become a multi-faceted participant?!

The following rate schedule is based on federally standardized costs for novel & short story characters (they are especially discounted for project members). Costs will vary based on a sliding scale of verifiable income level, personal relationship to author, monetary relationship to author (i.e. what he owes you from past favors, beers, etc.), authors needs, the pre-established glamor of your persona (but no one need be left out!):

$75—BASIC PACKAGE: Favorable peripheral character who adds color to background. Author develops character for you based on your auto-biographical sketch & profile response form. 1 line of conversation add $5.00, each additional line $1.00.

$250—FRIENDSHIP PACKAGE: Be a friend or ally of one of the designated main characters. Here's your chance to influence plot & careen through the story's steamy scenes! First 10 lines of conversation are free. Add $1 for every additional line over 10.

$500—CONSULTATION PACKAGE: Author consults YOU on your own character's idiosyncracies. Have a limp, an engraved ivory cane, or a special perversion. Be glamorous. Live in an upper Eastside penthouse. Be a Boho rocker complete with record deal, groupies & legacy of abuse. Follow the development. Be there at input level. (inc. all dialog & a la carte options.)

$1500—MAJOR CHARACTER PACKAGE: Be a full-fledged major character who dominates significant portions of action & actually determines destiny of the "I" character. 1 on 1 in-person consultations offer you chances to groom & edit. Includes everything: haircut, witty lines, interesting occupation, Trash & Vaudeville or Henri Bendel wardrobe, cultural literacy, adequate level of handsomeness & possibilities for advancement. (inc. all options.)

A LA CARTE OPTIONS: (included in CONSULTATION & MAJOR PACKAGES)

- **$75**—Interesting occupations: i.e. deep-sea diver, professional game show contestant, image makeover therapist, artisan, taste tester, private investigator, furniture stripper, etc.
- **$150**—Demi-monde occupation: stripper, dominatrix, gun runner, squatter, etc.
- **$69**—Be one of the many "real life" lover-researchers of the main "I" character. Price is for one night stand only. Add $7.50 for every additional "satisfying" tryst. Think you might be able to offer unique insights into "amour"? Be that wildly creative sexual co-conspirator with main "I" character for an additional $25.00. To be documented in novel add another $25.00.
- **$50**—For ample, mythic bosom (Diane Brill or Jayne Mansfield variety). Men add extra $25.00.
- **$10**—For nice legs. Men add extra $10.00.
- **$10**—For every piece of wisdom issued. Add $5.00 if a main character is influenced by your wisdom.

- **$25**—Ability to spout colorful post-beatnik jargon. Keep a beat, add $10. Make others laugh, add $8.95.
- **$10**—Suitable witty pseudonym based on your auto-bio sketch.

NO HANDS-ON CONTACT REQUIRED. ALTHO PHYSICAL CONTACT OPTIONS ARE AVAILABLE TO THOSE WHO QUALIFY. MEDICAL EXAM REQUIRED. MUST BE 18 & HAVE MAJOR CREDIT CARD.

Rates are REASONABLE, small down payment & reasonable payment plan. Use your unemployment benefits, food stamps, trust fund, or student loans to new effect. Empower yourself!

There are no hidden service charges. Your name will not be put on *Poets & Writers* mailing lists. Total confidentiality guaranteed (creative & entertaining pseudonyms supplied for nominal fee) & no serviceman or salesman will ever call. Your character copyright, of course, reverts back to you upon publication of participating novel. That's right, you can continue to play the character you developed in your own life.

You will also be eligible to join our Fictional Time Shares Portfolio which allows you to invest even further, beyond self-esteem enhancement & into an actual investment opportunity when this participatory novel is optioned for Film.

Yes, ACT NOW! Get in on ground floor. Still a number of exciting positions available. Novel quickly filling up. Become a legend with no mess, no fuss, no hidden clauses, no unmentioned diseases, no undesirable bodily fluid exchanges. Join Kurtz, Raskolnikov, Lolita, Cleopatra, Rhett Butler, Dr. Benway, Tess & Bartleby in the cavalcade of immortalized characters. No experience necessary. Write or Call Now for full prospectus, credentials & synopsis of the story that you will be participating in!

ALL AESTHETIC DECISIONS & LAST EDIT RIGHTS REMAIN THE AUTHOR'S. FULL REFUND AVAILABLE IF NOT SATISFIED. FORFEITURE OF ALL REFUND RIGHTS AFTER TEXT IS SENT TO PUBLISHER.▼

• bart plantenga fiction empowerment services inc. (b.p.f.e.s.i.)

FORENSIC SCIENCE VERIFIES AUTO-EROTICA

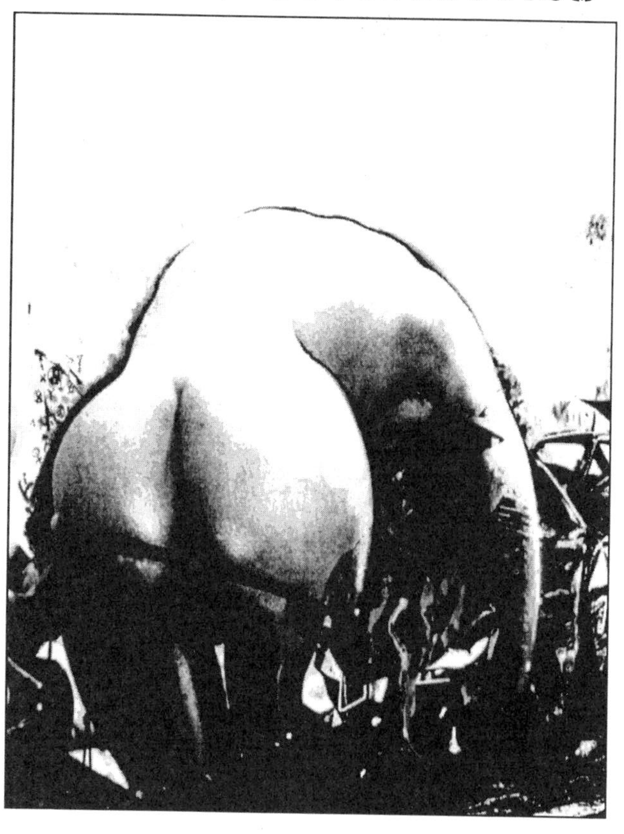

Shalom

> *...marrying through my own penis the car in which I had crashed.*
> • J.G. Ballard

SECTION 1: SITES OF REVERIE:

The mangled transport vehicle wrecks were installed at strategic points around the city to help re-invest the general populace with a certain fervor. Periodic shopping squalls & localized consumption frenzies, though, seemed to be the sole instincts revitalized by our Collision Dolmen Proposal.

This had not been the original intent of its architects, & now commercial sponsorship was threatening to undermine all our goals. Major hyper-market ad reps assured us that spotlights & rotating platforms would enhance the visual effect of each wreck.

Tourists had already discovered them as Photo Opportunities. This usually entailed subjects be posed in mock crash scenarios next to the gruesome wrecks. This made them laugh, & few things made people laugh anymore. Psychopathologists referred to the wrecks as "vital sublimation stations," though latent societal superstitions kept most from crawling inside the wrecks.

Suicide Rates—epecially vehicular—had shot up alarmingly in recent years, & seemed to be indifferent to both sociological factors & peaks of consumptive splurging. 3-television households seemed especially vulnerable.

The original goal of our Proposal had been to somehow re-balance the scales of fervor back toward the once-reigning Fear-Of-Death notion. Tipping them away from the rather disturbing decade-long rash we called, affectionately enough, "The Fear-Of-Life-Dynamic."

The particular collision to which I was daily drawn, in a less than professional capacity, I must say, had become much more than a mere monument to our own tenuous mortality. This particular torsion sculpture had, for me, become a talisman of both pain & grace.

Several of the vehicle's body panels—the right rear, for instance—had somehow managed to remain free of the usual extrusion striations. This perversely unscathed area had somehow remained oblivious to the scream of tangled steel, that final cluster of frantic thoughts. It reminded me of a pearl-handled dagger I once saw protruding from the belly of a long dead dog.

The haughty gleam on these panels revealed her face—& not mine. This is how we met & that was enough. I didn't need to touch the panels to touch her—at least not at first.

I only began to truly touch & polish these rear panels when it was already too late. A week after our first encounter, I discovered a cinderblock on the curb. It had, during one noxious crepuscule, finished off the last winking glimmers of her foremost perfection.

All the remaining glass had been shattered with bricks, from a pile where once had stood a plant with humming machines that made things people didn't need anymore. All the wheels were gone too. I, though, in a tic of prescience, had managed to salvage one of her exquisite spoke wire hubs only 2 days earlier. I had it mounted to spin freely on an iron bar. It mesmerized me, like a pinwheel does a child, & afforded me temporary access to a more contemplative universe.

I sometimes imagined what I'd do to the young trash thugs with their glands drenched in rampaging hormones. The kind who get all bitter & jittery around beauty which mocks the counterfeit echoes in their empty lives.

During the day the panels gathered sun—the same sun that hung over Venice, Venice, Italy, *her* Venice. Sometimes I read the weather reports for Venice. Tried to imagine what she might wear today. The latest pink satin bellbottoms? The kind only Prince was brave enough to wear. Or whether she dreamt of being someone she wasn't, someone she'd never thought of before.

I spent all my accumulated vacation days here, with one hand on her trunk. During the summer the panels would stay warm well past midnight.

It must be stated at this point that before this particular investigation I had had no predisposition toward aberrant sexual enticement, nor was I much of a connoisseur of vintage road transport. & I'd always scoffed at roadway romantics who sought to make movies & martyrs of the "victims".

Her body had indeed been provocative. Perhaps too generous with gifts of beauty, too much for the kind of man who had bought her—& then apparently killed her. Oh, what the prick does to the heart! He of the kind who buys fidelity like one purchases a book that'll never be read.

Her cunt could've been prized, like a kid's mitten or a small coin purse. I remember the cut of her bells. I remember her body, laid out perfect on the medical examiner's stainless steel table. I remember wanting to give her a pillow, & then seeing the blood-soaked towel around her head. I remember the plastic Virgin Mary dash ornament, embedded—nay, nearly totally enveloped by the fatty facial tissue—the way pudding sucks up a dropped spoon. I remember him probing the elegantly trimmed tuft of wishbone hair like I remember the nosegay from my senior ball. I remember the examiner saying, "evidence of seminal fluid."

Behind us her tattered but stylish clothing hung in the air to dry. Periodically, I heard fragments fall from the cling of the fabric to the brown paper on the floor, especially positioned there to catch any minute granules of evidence.

My periodic foray into coarseness like this is merely a technique designed to mitigate my nausea & sorrow. Emotional entanglements are very much frowned upon in this business, especially with a numinous body like hers. Just as my father had taught me on the farm not to name animals being fattened for slaughter. Dogs, yes. Pigs, no. It had been some time since I'd been allowed to be tender. A thick skin is certainly prized around here. It's essential. I'd become somewhat of a crash-scene-cowboy; a legend, I dare say. I was not averse to putting my hand inside a gaping wound. I'd become known for my spurs & for the way my sharp tongue could whittle down any ornery street drood in seconds flat.

The desperation of everything, including pre-paid status, manifests itself in funny ways. Take the vehicle's almost ludicrously non-functional trunk. Or the interior details done in antelope bone. But then again all this, this luxury, reminded me of her. & the resistance to function had been made noble by her. She too had preferred aesthetics to function.

At first I didn't think I'd ever open her trunk again, after that night of the initial investigation. I remember the hot crack of camera flashes lighting up the sky like quivers of heat lightning. & with my hand & face deep inside her trunk I'd realized that this was no ordinary investigation. They or he or she had been someone. The 2 hi-powered rifles were quickly impounded.

I remember the right tail light, its warmth penetrating my trouser leg.

Being designated a "Collision Dolmen"—like some forelorn Stonehenge—then removing a wreck from its "natural" setting & installing it in its locale was meant to enhance its "dramatis sculpturis". & over the weeks I must've looked quite the sight, standing by her trunk, opening & closing, opening & closing it, mesmerized by its craftsmanship & how it resembled the way her elbows must've worked. Few people ventured here then. The site had been chosen without proper psycho-geographic analysis. It had not been located near a major rush hour artery. It was positioned near an off-ramp that led nowhere, with scavenger birds hovering over the shallow grey surfaces & cement depressions.

This suited me just fine. While squat monks & skateboarders congregated at the sites of police cruiser crashes, & sports fans flocked to the charred automotive carcasses of fanatically re-tooled racing machines, I remained by her side, content to not have to share her with anyone. Cinephiles made their pilgrimages to the newly restored (in some cases crassly re-created) wreckages of James Dean's '51 Porsche & Jayne Mansfield's '66 Lincoln. There were those who were negotiating with the estate of Harry Chapin to use his blue Rabbit along the Long Island Expressway. Bessie Smith's scandalous auto death had recently been reconstructed, despite the

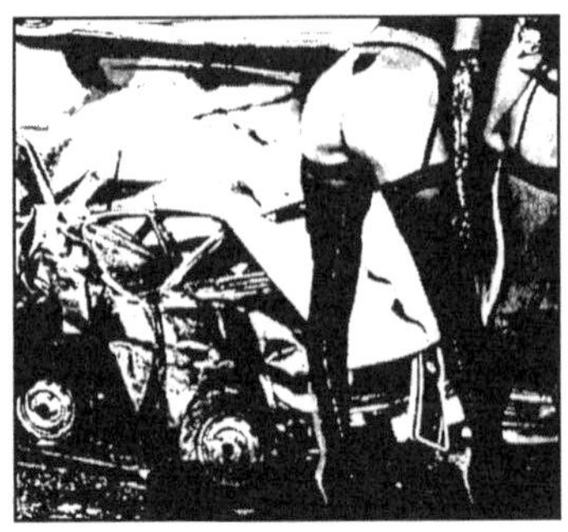

protests of white supremacists. It seemed as if every demographic group had developed their own very distinctive tastes/needs in collision megaliths, just as they had for beer or jam.

One day I discovered a tour group around my site. It made me anxious. A herd of driver-education trainees led by their conceited guide, a bespectacled M.A. in Crash Science. He relished pointing out small details—tufts of hair, fabric impressions, blood-spray patterns. Yet, her blood type didn't seem to matter to HIS type, & the fact that the once-white bucket seats were now blood brown brought odd smirks to his face.

He was proud of this crash, like a jazz aficianado is proud of his rare Ellington. He was prone to issuing rather facile proclamations, things that were meant only to attach status to his person. He went through great pains to come up with the most hackneyed & pathetic allusions, often comparing the wreck to scenes in Homer's *Odyssey*, or to the haunting nature of bleached human skulls in the killing fields.

He also liked to act as if he had mastered all her conundrums. He spoke with particular confidence about speed at impact, sensory impairment & skid-mark patterns. It was as if he were bragging about his own daughter at a reunion.

I resented his well-groomed effeteness. I sneered like a jealous suitor at the nameplate pinned to his lapel. I withdrew into a cozy haven of wrath. My allusions to packs of tourists & gang rape could hardly be suppressed. I vowed to change my visitation hours to dodge his. As they say: twice burned, thrice shy. & as others say: never burned, never cry.

In fact, he carried on as if she were HIS! Patted her bumper in the silliest, most sexist manner. & yet, had he ever tried her glove-box? If he had truly cared he'd have found a way in. But he was just an instructor, after all! & those who can't do, teach. & those who can't teach become cops, enforcing unenforceable laws they themselves don't have the capacity to comprehend.

Had he ever taken the time to pay homage to things we can never know? Gather small souvenirs, fragments, windshield crystals the size of teeth, to compose a kind of postmortem biography? Did he help remove evidentiary fragments from her facial epidermis? No, no, & no.

Had he ever been aware of acute eroto-synesthesia from the mere handling of her personal effects? No. His arousal mechanics were totally circumscribed by the exchange of currency for services rendered. 18.7% of all Americans have known mental disorders.

SECTION 2: Selected Data & the Quantifiable Transmogrification of Collision Damage.

A. The transport vehicle.

The Ferrari xpi-6a, priced at $112,000.00 had been totalled. Totalled should NOT rule out the potential for salvage, however. Salvage is the art of the scavenger. Souvenir is the French word for memento. [She breathed heavily & I knew immediately that her soul was twice the size of the Ferrari's drive train.]

1. front bumper wrapped like a pinch around the guard rail post.

2. front fenders crushed, accordion-style. [Or the folds of her belly with forehead to knees.]

3. paint-flake spectograph analysis of the 15-coat alkyd-resin process revealed no foreign friction marks along side panels, voiding a sideswipe scenario. [I watched her nails—same red as the Ferrari's—peel off my shirt. "The collar's frayed," she said, without hint of haughtiness.]

4. headlight assembly: impellent fragments of sealed-beam Pyrex

revealed speed at impact of 87 mph. Crystals found jettisoned 31 yards from scene of initial impact. [My hands got caught in her breathing knots of flaming hair.]

5. headlight filament examination determined that headlights were on at moment of impact. [*April In Paris* by Sarah Vaughn with Clifford Brown.]

6. tire analysis revealed no foul play punctures nor evidence of prior deficient repair or blow out, i.e. frayed bore hole. [Sheet music flew around the room. We were breathing out of ideas.]

7. brakes: metal fatigue not evident after extensive metallurgical structural deficiency tests. [Bloated whispers full of moisture.]

B. Scene of Collision.

1. vehicle positioned at 12° off perpendicular. The weather & coefficient of friction failed to supply cause of accident.

2. roadway's extremely curved course, however, revealed possible transgressive factor. Perhaps locale was chosen to mask homicide-suicide. Skid marks were lengthy but revealed no true arc, implying there had been no effort made to steer out of the vehicle's course.

3. position of driver: facing passenger. Backbone shattered by impact with roof beam.

4. position of passenger: facing driver, right side of head crushed & Virgin Mary dash ornament found embedded in right cheek.1/3 of body ejected from compartment due to abrupt deceleration. Urine traces found soaked into lush padding of passenger seat. (I have one of her incisors, which I found embedded in the leather dash, in a tea cup in my home.) Superficial ear & facial tissue found on projecting details & wiper mounts. (She stared at me like a broken window.)

5. clothing: torn blouse matched fibers found under driver's fingernails. Possible evidence of struggle. Strap-less Lejaby azure lace bra discovered down at her waist. Lipstick: nouvelle rouge piano #26 impressions found on sleeve of driver's shirt. Ashtray contained 7 lengthy filtered Rothman cigarette butts with lipstick traces. Only

4 had lipstick traces that matched her lipstick. 3 butts had lipstick traces of another shade, another source, another woman. Pink bell-bottoms revealed zipper from navel to tail of backbone. Her panties were of fine manufacture & functionally crotchless. (& breathing full of breath.)

C. Glovebox Revelations.

1. contents removed carefully in order in which they occurred from the top. AAA info; leather driving glove (seldom worn); driver's license of one John M. Lehrman; maps of Las Vegas, Florida, Guatemala. Car insurance documents reveal discrepancies in driver's name: John N. Lernman.

2. document #1 reveals one John N. Lehman as co-author of an Army Field Strategy Pamphlet entitled *KING OF THE HILLS,* which explains, in basic Dick & Jane language, the strategy & rules of playing King of the Hill. Incorporates fluid battlefield tactics & 22 color graphics. (Cost to taxpayer; $103,000.00)

3. Document #2: *MEDICAL TREATISE OF CHASTICAL REMEDIES TO PRESERVE MORALITY IN DEBTOR NATIONS;* a. authored by one James M. Loemann. (Cost to taxpayer; $96,000.00) Purpose: to set equatorial nations on the path to moral responsibility, industriousness & solvency. Pushed through by the powerful banking lobby to force debtor nations to make good on their loans. Among the manual's recommendations on how to alleviate idleness & overpopulation:

a. reasons must be detailed & corroborated by any available means: i.e. excessive masturbation & indiscriminate fornication causes weakened morality, diminished patriotism, homosexuality, memory loss, epilepsy, imbecility & acne.

b. female chastity belt patent #438,439; girdle consists of padded cushions designed to fit around the vulva with special grating of animal bone which allows urine to pass. Apparatus hooked together by series of pulley belts to pair of tight trousers, secured by padlock. Bilingual instructions for possible indigenous manufacture.

c. clitorechtomies: for extreme cases of wantonness. Curbs desire. Increases work place productivity.

d. unisex bio-beta chastity device. Electrodes applied to genitalia. Short circuits desire. No discernible nausea or physical discomfort. Product of BioBapTek, BBT, a Baptist-owned behavior-modification firm.

e. chastity belt patent #563,882 with adjustable contoured tube for male member. Perforated tip allows urination. Inside, protruding pricking points issue painful warnings when erection occurs. Perfect for wet dream eradication.

f. castration: often a necessary tactic to regain household solvency. Easy-to-follow tri-lingual diagrams for out-patient, in-home application.

D. Follow-Up Data.

1. psycho-profile of driver: revealed official documentation of scopophilia (obsession with sight of genitalia) treatment. Skeptical employer, the U.S. State Dept., ponders if he may not be security risk. Regional reassignment request petitioned for on very day of his death.

2. cogent backdrop material: revealed potentially embarassing conflict of interest questions between government contractors & State Dept. officials.

3. recent details of driver's liaisons with one Sophia Piquanti, the deceased passenger, had been leaked to the press.

4. Ms. Piquanti had been purported lover of various mobsters & dictator's sons. Also had been "personal secretary" of Charlton Heston several months in 1985. Background Documents stated: "what she knew Marilyn Monroe knew too."

5. driver's marriage of 21 years dissolving in face of revelations.

6. driver had recently completed TV spot for American Express. His classic handsomeness earned him nickname, "James Bond of Encino."

7. driver had recently stated to a reporter, "I'm America's #1

patriot, but right now I've been made to feel more like roadkill, like carrion being picked clean."

8. driver had recently accepted clemency assurances from the House Committee On Unethical Foreign Intervention for his valued testimony on William Casey's purported chemically-induced "brain tumor," money laundering, the chastity fiasco, evangelical mercenaries trained by the Marines, rock stars used (sometimes unwittingly) to promote Third World castration policies, & Coca Cola spiked with sterilization chemicals.

9. interesting studies of "the delayed effects of military service on subsequent mortality; a randomized experiment." The chief finding was of excess post-discharge mortality from motor vehicle injuries [E810-E827, International Classification of Diseases] & suicide [E950-E959, ICD, 8th Revision] among uniformed soldier group (Korean Vets, Vietnam Vets, Desert Storm Troops, National Guardsmen & Vets from the Panama & Grenada campaigns) as compared with the civilian control group.

E. Purse Contents of Ms. Piquanti.

1. 2 Tall Girl insoles for falling arches.
2. 3 reservoir-tipped Lambinda brand lambskin prophylactics.
3. eyeliner: "*harmonie nacree d'ombre*" by Lancôme.
4. 2 losing California Lotto tickets.
5. various make-up devices & emory boards.
6. tear gas cannister by On-Gard.
7. bottle of Heroin(e) *Parfum*.
8. copy of *The Decameron* by Boccacio, in Italian.
9. shopping list: included products incongruous with her social position, such as frozen pizza & lo-cal ice milk.
10. identification: Sophia Piquanti, born: Venice, Italy; home: Cherry Hill, NJ; height: 5'8"; weight: 113 lbs.; occupation: model; birthdate: 6.19.59; eyes: blue-green. Driver's license issued from state of California.
11. veterinarian appointment for cat identified as "Pipi": needed panleukopenia & rhinotracheitis shots. Note requested Ms.

Piquanti bring along stool sample.

12. Document: "Tall Girl Quadruple Width Shoes, A Diary Entry:"

I was 16. Breathing out of yearning. Under an overpass. Carroll Gardens, Brooklyn. Late. Where cars speed by like birds with terrified calls. It's where guys dump cars in the Gowanus Canal to collect insurance.

I couldn't date Barry anymore. Too many strange calls. I saw HEADLIGHTS ON HI BEAM, & minutes later it was dark like the inside of a cheap coat. He released me & said, "I love you. I wanted to kiss you but I knew you had a scar." SOUND OF CAR HORN OUTSIDE 3 TIMES. I didn't know why.

"I knew something had turned you against men."

"Oh, Barry." I murmured.

"Will you marry me?" he asked, tightening his factory-trained mechanic's arms around my quivering waist.

"Yes, Barry, yes!" I cried inside my pants. Accepting to spite my own best interests.

THE DOMELIGHT WENT ON & OFF & ON. & again I didn't know why. I thought perhaps it was something bigger than the both of us, & the moon revolved around him.

"Boy, I'm gonna think I dreamed all this." He said. "I'm gonna marry a gorgeous figure & she's ALL mine!" As the BRAKE-LIGHTS FLICKERED SPORADICALLY the word suddenly seemed like a slap in the face. What gorgeous figure? Was he thinking of someone else? I didn't say word. I had already tried creams, exercises, suction devices, therapy, everything I could think of to improve my bust. But nothing worked. Flat I was & flat I'd stay. Someone outside OPENED THE CAR HOOD, CLOSED IT WITH A SLAM. It seemed to amplify my pulse. I got so nervous about my figure that when Barry put his arms around me I'd jerk away. With RADIO ON MAXIMUM VOLUME—SOMEONE CHANGED THE STATION. I wouldn't even let him kiss me, afraid he'd find out about my figure.

"Hey, I can wait till we're married, if you prefer, but you don't have to jerk away like a scared rabbit!" Barry said as SOMEONE

FOLDED A FRONT SEAT FORWARD & BACK WITH A GREAT SENSE OF URGENCY 4 TIMES.

"If you don't like the way I jump, then don't hold me," I snapped. Barry stormed out. I ran upstairs. Threw myself across my bed & sobbed my heart out. & vowed to stay locked in my room forever. Mom heard me, came in & said; Beverly I know you were wearing padded bras." SOMEONE OUTSIDE RUNS A FOREFINGER ALONG FENDERS, THEN IDLY FLICKS SIDE TRIM. "You should have come to me sooner," she said.

SECTION 3: Clash of Doubt & Dream.

Did the crash prof—he's just a driving instructor instructor, afterall—ever wonder why automobiles were black until the 1940s? Or how a car's tires can build up a tremendous static charge of thousands of volts? No!

Did he ever wonder how Pasolini died in '75? Did he know a cheap male whore had run over his body, over & over & then driven away with the radio on, only to receive a light sentence because of Pasolini's unsavory lifestyle & politics. No!

Didn't he pretend to know the lay of this concrete expanse? Where the young *sans abri* needed heat, which led them to set fire to cars? Where they ate small rodents. & that to them the rodents tasted not unlike fried chicken from picnics they remembered.

He—with his toupée, his credit cards, his air conditioning, his casual indifference—how could HE know this obtuse quadrangle had become a crucible of white noise, a field of battle, a scarred turf with rusted skeletons whose former function now escaped us? A senseless meridian of unfinished concrete tombs & noseless statuary lost to history, caught in a swirl of styrofoam & dust, where squat monks, art gypsies & opiate athletes had once roamed & reigned freely. Where they now cracked open the coiled copper entrails of discarded air conditioners & frigos & sucked out the freon to get altered, get re-fitted into a more fantastic mindscape.

Sure, one could see the dead whelps, mongrels with bloated guts, carcasses picked clean by blowflies & mutts with mangy pelts as ratty as any 20-year old throw rug. If one had been looking! But how would one measure the density of dead dogs? Aerial photography? How could he or anyone know that progress had somehow gone inside out long ago? Like a drunk praying in a pit toilet, puking up intestines, which look just like grimy socks full of holes wrapped around knuckles.

Did he know that thousands of us were dreaming of *chiens*—when dreams came to us at all—dreams of terrifying pariahs with insolent mugs; like the hounds of hell guarding our chicken coops with their foaming mouths & piercing eyes, roaming across cement fields & tarps of shade in baneful packs. No, he could not know how these dreams had changed our dispositions, our posture, our mistrust of everything concrete or metaphysical. Our dreams were just perverse eyeliner for the soul, outlining the fear that street dogs had wrought.

Coming face to face with canine djinns, these new hyper-clairvoyant *chiens*, we grip the weighted umbrellas we never seem to leave at home anymore. Our hands sweat & ache.

This was the year of the Dog in the Chinese Calendar, when they began to eat this fear of ours, to sow it ever deeper & deeper, to reap it with all the gusto they had once reserved for gnawing away at neckbones. They had, in fact, begun their ascension in this, their year, already reigning over whole peripheral swaths of the city.

The inner cities still served as bastions of hyper-wealth, where portfolioed souls bolstered their existences with the re-tooled nostalgia of pasts they'd never had. From these clime-controlled enclaves periodic regional safety quotients were issued. These figures regulated the price of real estate, affecting the morose migrations of dreamless souls.

& all the hearses in the enclaves & outbacks were indeed still as black as they'd always been. "Black is black," said the newspapers, quoting the lyrics of pop songs with all their characteristic tautological smugness. & some youngster, a fortunate discard along the funeral procession, drained of all dream & hope, suggested that ambulances should be painted black too. It would make everything a lot simpler & quicker, he said.

POSTSCRIPT.

My mom, months after, took me to the scene of the other crash. She showed me the skid marks. She thought it amazing that the marks were still there. She picked up automotive debris that had so long ago been tossed over the guard rail. She lugged it around with her. She wanted to take a headlight housing with her. I told her to put it down. I had to snatch it from her grip & toss it down the steep incline myself. I hadn't seen her like this, so animated, so excited, in a very long time, not since my parents' 25th wedding anniversary, or my brother's first wedding.

Then we drove to my dad's car which sat, crushed like a beer can, out back of the Downsville Sunoco. & there we stood, remembering family vacations. Remembering the way sweat dripped from the end of his nose & sizzled on the hot engine block as he fiddled with the carburetor. She cried. We touched the areas of his car that had perhaps touched him. "It's a miracle that he's recovering. He says it's my cooking."

On the way home she asked if I was OK. "Yea." But I wasn't. A handful of windshield crystal I'd scooped from the floorboard of what was left of his car into my backpocket dug into my skin. I had read how the despondent (but not too despondent to not want to save the feelings of loved ones) wrapped suicides in the gift wrap of automotive accident.

"Are you sure?"

"Yea." ▼

THE GG—1 SERIES OF MODEL POSES

Jonathon Rosen

Aviators wearing T-shirts that declare, "Women Are Property"
• Michael R. Gordon, *NY Times*

THE 4x5 poses displayed here feature Joan, the 1983 B&G Queen in the State Dept. *Bondage Annual,* & Lois, our "Silk Stocking Siren" of some 40 Foreign Policy Trade Agreement films. Lois is shown here in her patented snug-fit bras, detailed with brass grommets & posed with the Chrysler R-1 tank & U.S. manufactured fast food containers. The photos show, it is reported, the 1987 Malaysian Commerce Consortium on their feet demanding more.

SVELTE Sigrid here is featured in our martial arts video, which highlights developments in counter-insurgency techniques. Bonus 4x5 leggy poses of her bound body have already found their way into some of the innermost sanctums of the world's Commerce Monarchies, where *"revolution"* is reserved for the realm of coiffures & pleats.

DINING regulations & the placement of silverware have of late begun, in fact, to reflect these changing economic realities, as is clearly evidenced in a number of our 4x5 poses at $.40 ea.

NOTICE the new binding cord in these 4x5 bound & gagged poses. Made of the finest Army-gauge rip-stop nylon. In extensive Female-Recruit Tests the cord showed below normal bruise counts & exceptionally low allergic skin abrasion figures, as noted by feminists who mounted a strong media campaign to have the outmoded hemp-based binding material replaced by the more humane nylon.

& FOR your eruditional tittilation Joan & Lois wear Ralph Lauren's new prêt-à-porter copies of antique American chains & shackles as worn by actual Chatanooga slaves.

ALSO available are 15 spanking poses utilizing the very effective yet very safe open-hand technique. 12 of which feature our blond,

Lois, in tight deSade-inspired corsets. These are NOT for the faint of heart however. Nor for those who refuse to believe poetry is dead & refuse to acknowledge that, at 25, most poets opt for writing ad copy that tends to arouse affairs of the wallet & not the heart.

14 NEW hi-heel poses at $.40 ea. feature allusions to more savage worlds. Furlined panties in 6 are known to moderate 7 categories of Repudemocretin anxiety. The rest feature our models in garish lipstick (as recommended by J. Helms' study, *Prurient Minutiae & Seductive Variables*) & stockings with lengthy runs. Enclosed literature reveals how to follow the runs on the upstroke—from ankle to thigh—to maximize resultant stimulation of spurious dining in establishments which feature men with small repetitive vocabularies.

IN 12% of known cases, rapid repetition of limited vocabularies does not simulate mantras, if anything, it has been increasingly implicated in stimulating latent gunfire memories. For these cases we feature 10 poses of our raven-haired Lillian, veteran Annette Funicello stand-in in "Beach Blanket Burn Baby Burn" & star of "Furious Fighting Damsels." She is shown here (with Patrick Buchanan behind her jestfully lunging his pelvis with a bayonet hilariously emerging from his open gold-plated fly) provocatively picking up dropped silverware. This usually helps focus on spinal dissimulation, configurations of gestural submission & forgotten chakras. The carpet is of a thick US-manufactured revolutionary photo-sensitive Congolite® pile fiber.

THE FF-1 series features hi-heeled Lillian in scanty attire posing with key hi priority words that resonate until most chandeliers begin to shiver. This documented phenomenon usually alleviates 92% of all moral qualms in the public sector & opens up new roads to heightened consumer stimuli.

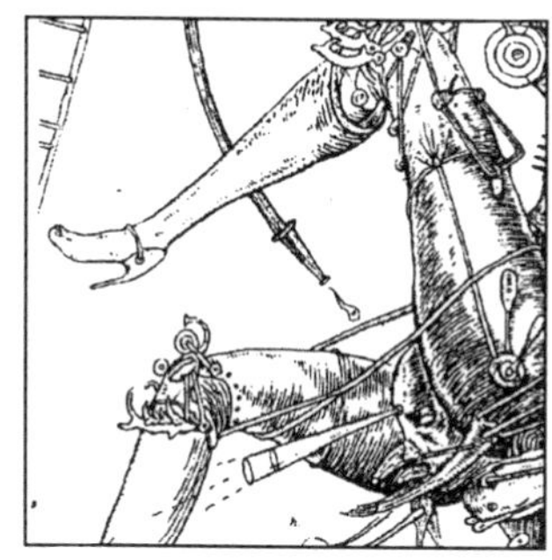

AS CUES, these potent *langue*-bites are smartly embroidered on Lillian's stocking tops. Although some of the poses feature rough & tumble, hi-spirited hair pulling between Lillian & Sigrid, the words are ALWAYS plainly visible. Maximized climax is absolutely guaranteed with these poses at $.40 ea.

28 CONTROVERSIAL new poses at $.50 ea. procured under the Freedom of Information Act feature selected press conferences utilizing the aforementioned embroidered cues. The cues are large & always legible but, convenient to State Dept. policy, continue to diminish in meaning, proving that essential Oval Office axiom that the less one has to say the more one should be encouraged & sponsored to say it.

DETAILS of Reagan's Cerebral Death in 1982 have absolutely NO verified bearing on the dimensions & resonance of his Michael Jackson speech, his Duke = Disney Equations (a prescient speech that predicted Disney's hiring of David Duke away from Coors®), or his frequent aircraft carrier allusions made in late 1984.

IN SEVERAL speeches the 4x5s reveal Reagan undergoing electroprobe stimulation. Still others, never before available to the public reveal constant neuro-stimul-erotic prompting by the comely offspring of ex-Nazi Intelligence experts escorted into America after WW II.

THESE Germanic gals have voluntarily foregone promising mudwrestling careers for Stero-cortisonal bosom enhancement in the National Interest, to parade in sup-hose & whalebone corsets from Alaska with Reagan-Bush-Duke-Helms speeches neatly stencilled on their corsets. The poses reveal Reagan flanked by his manifestly semi-tumescent National Security Advisors. These promptings reveal the ever-delicate nature of National Security decision-making.

HALF of the Army chiefs-of-staff shown dining here with entertainment & fragrance industry representatives, clearly show erectile tension ranging from 23% to 81% in their well-creased slacks after being aroused by a gunpowder-based frangrance, "Shellshock" worn by our Joan, though secret polls now in our possession revealed that the staff STILL prefered carpet bombing to cunnilingus.

THE Fragrance Feasability Test aroused more rhythmic EKG stimulation in cerebrum-dead Reagan (as well as in labia-phobic Falwell) than in any other single event, other than his vaunted priapic invasion of Grenada. Before his death, Ray Kroc, in an initiative of supplementary patriotism, had post-operative priapic-tissue-transplant Reagan sign into law a military beautification & privatization bill requiring ALL US-manufactured bombs & rockets be hand-painted with "the colorful characters of Ronald McDonaldland®." Disney-Duke Studios® (where the hooded KKK merges with the be-capped 7 dwarves) have matched these McKroc sums & will further "undrab & de-traumatize" much of our larger Naval hardware (Mediterranean Cruisers, Destroyers & Aircraft Carriers) with the signature Disney iconography to show, in the words of Disney PAC spokesperson, Gennifer Flowers, that "military hardware is an extension of our national smile."

IN 12 exclusive top secret 4x5s just made available at $.75 ea., Jim Henson creator of the Muppets®, flanked by our leggy models—setting aside his Liberconmanian Party loyalties—is shown accepting the task of "recreating Reagan in a likeness more real than he ever was himself."

OUR provocative models in the KK-1 series were subsequently hired by the State Dept. to do Holidays On Ice® with the Muppet characters & spent countless hours dubbing their pleasant & perky voices into the Henson-built readily-identifiable American icons. The poses feature our busty, thinly-clad DumDum® models on the ice with steroid-enhanced Bulkan No-neck Wrestlers, driving home the State Department's message that "embracing stylish anti-militarism not only undermines our socio-economic stability but American family values as well."

THIS, then, is my feeble attempt, as a Repudemocretin State Department sub-operative, to expose to you the clandestine goings-on in behind the Federal Green Door, in hopes that this deep throat exposé will in some way atone for my involvement, & will perhaps allow you to see me in a less unfavorable light should these revelations lead to a Federal Inquisition. ▼

THE WOMAN WITH ONE TOO MANY FACES

Mag Bee

> ***I was the first woman to burn her bra. It took the fire department 4 days to put it out.***
> **• Dolly Parton**

Liz Taylor (in Tennessee Williams' *Boom* looking like a self-absorbed Cleopatra pushing a shopping cart through an Acme): "Your voice, it vibrates in my ears not so much like a voice as like a sensation."

Richard Burton (looking like royalty trying for beatnik chic): "You'll make me as vain as a peacock if you go on like this, & I have to keep the humility of my faith."

Liz (swooning): "Is this, then...a time for kissing? (No-nonsense kiss) Aaaah...unnnh...thank you."

Richard: "A woman doesn't usually thank a man for kissing her, especially when she's so lovely—& owns an island."

Liz: "I have lots of art treasures—including myself."

Renee (real name Debbie Dudley—twirled baton in high school marching band) liked me because I was a natural ham. Said I looked like Victor Mature in his prime.

When you get to her chicken shack (somewhere west of Trenton, east of Salt Lake City; by referral only) she hands you a gilded velveteen menu, from which you select: "appetizer," a quickie, a 3 minute rock video, a 60 second ad; "entree a la carte," 2 hours, a film; "full-course meal," all night, a lifetime of sorts.

After you make a selection she hands you a script. Expects you to learn it as you wait in her satin parlor. I had the stuff pretty much up in my head. I'm Renee's regular regular.

All her scripts are neatly transcribed from videos, which she sagaciously studies in her library screening room.

I'd usually call her from down the road a piece. Put in my order, so's she could be ready. I knew what I liked & she liked that...

Hitchhiking hooked me with Big Bad John (isn't that every legend's name?) who taught me a whole lot of whatever: Pick-ups, truck routes, slaughterhouse details—how he hit cattle between the eyes with a sledgehammer—sailor knots, troubleshooting.

But not *trust, apparently. Thus I have this diary fragment, ripped pages grabbed at random while BB John, Peterbilt 16-wheeling Odysseus, was out getting some greasy take-out.*

Was it courage? Something to write home about? Don't know. I didn't have much to lose anyway; a p.o. box, a Chevelle up on blocks, some records.

BB John was a timebomb, a handsome myth about to happen, a sinewy Popeye with veins that popped in his forehead when he spoke. He was tanned, stone chiseled, impatient with rolled-up tee shirt sleeves. Even limped like Gene Vincent. Unattached without being detached, married without rigor mortis.

His truck cabin contained hundreds of cassettes strewn about, cig ash wafting about, boxes & bags of half-eaten somethings. Rubbery monster things dangled & wiggled. His centerpiece, a jiggly hula dancer with the Virgin Mary's head grafted to it, adequately revealed his notions of religion.

His sneaky kid smile was like a basement door that lets the light in. I'm still trying to imitate it. But lie to him—like when they'd "neglected" to tell him he was transporting nuclear waste from Houston to Idaho—& the smile turned suddenly sinister.

& he could talk about anything: cars, Bangkok, interplanetary travel, the Iroquois False Face Society, Alaskan flora, or the music of Jimmy Dean & George Jones. I remember the cassettes, him cranking them up so that I'd get the lyrics.

When he pushed through a flytrap screendoor people looked up from their games, dreams & plates. A unique amalgam of attitude & movement, a haughty swagger in a halo of smoke. & if he got inside a story he'd use both hands to pull you in. Eyes on—& beyond—like buttons that burned flesh. I hadn't thought his stories anything but stories, a way to pass time, make the miles come easier, until, tucked away in Golden Gate Park, I actually read the wad of diary. & there & then I realized that most of his underbelly adventures were just too fantastic not to be true. He left me off near Gillette, Wyoming, & forever thereafter—even today—I think every truck nosing the ridge, making a wide left is him coming back to "re-educate my face," as he'd put it. It was at the moment I climbed down out of his cab with the diary wad down my pants that I joined the adult world, a world where a goodbye never means a simple goodbye. Every knife became double-edged. Every conversation fraught with barbs & double meaning.

Renee Sagittaire was the *nom de plume* of a bitch savior of aimless souls in search of plot. Like a switchboard operator connecting us with our souls, lost to weariness & worry. Shrewd entrepreneur? Yes, & clean as a nun's whistle too.

To be with her was like rubbing your nose into a big perfumey mum head. Henry Miller'd need a trilogy of a thousand pages to get her down. She's known as "The Woman of a Thousand Faces." I swear on god's bare ass I've never seen her REAL face. But if she's gone to these lengths, making masks that fit like surgical gloves, like dreams, then who'm I to unmask her? Because ANY way she is, is real to me. & that's bottom dollar what counts. Life's all images we either decide to spit out or swallow.

I'm a surface sorta guy. Call it survival if you want. So if I'm watching her Rita Hayworth do her caustic bump & grind in black satin, noir whisper, the kind of strip that had churches nationwide scrambling to denounce her, I'm with her on her way to hell. I'm lucky in a world where surveillance shrink-wraps the dream.

If anything, Renee is enthusiasm in the flesh, & enthusiasm's how Renee got into this dream factory. & it was my enthusiasm for her enthusiasm—as Gloria Swanson says, playing a DeMille Babylonian princess in peacock Ra headdress accented by farflung rays of pearl and stretches of shimmering skin—that led her down the yellow brick road to who knows what kind of redemption.

She's probably done a thousand faces since '74. Updates her selections constantly. Keeps them trendy. Today there's no Mama Cass, Ali McGraw, Patti Page, Britt Ekland, or Sharon Tate. Replaced by Madonna, Christie Brinkley, Kirstie Alley, LaToya Jackson, Isabella Rosellini & Darryl Hannah.

While many faces change, just as many remain the same. Peggy Lee is still there & goes for a little extra. She was one of my first, helping dredge up some good memories of my father. He had autographed glossies of her he kept hidden from my mother. I used to call her "Piggy Leak" to tease him. It's only when I see Renee decked out in a breathless crepe dress warbling "Fever" in slutty club style that I begin to understand the true sensuality of blasé.

Perennial faves like Annette Funicello in a Mouseketeers' cap, or in a cumbersome 50s bikini that gallantly muzzles her brimming plenitude (a bosom that had sent seismic tremors of alarm through Walt Disney's schematic notion of life) seemed to have second winds, 9 lives. So while Patty Hearst & Jessica Hahn each lasted 2 months on her menu, the likes of Tina Turner are approaching their second decade of popularity.

& Turner's the one you want if you want to look like you just came out of a brawl with a unique configuration of black & blue. Or you can nestle in the classic fertile valley of Dolly Parton. Or Jane Russell's, while listening to her lecture on proper foundations, showing off her famous "second story balcony," modeling bras designed by the aeronautical bosom buff, Howard Hughes.

Renee could play these fullsome [*sic*] brabusters to the nipple, manipulating the mystique that is the awesome beauty of the bosom, which as the source of fixation & fetish intimidates both sexes out of serious camraderie. She isolated a central cultural dread, women who had, for far too long, depended on cleavage for personality, & men who'd confused tit-fixation for affection. Yea, there's drama amongst all that delight.

Renee had her own stable of faves. They tended to stretch her dramatic skills: Garbo, Dietrich, Bardot, Louise Brooks, Francis Farmer (on & off screen), Susan Hayward, Maureen O'Sullivan, Carmen Miranda, Josephine Baker, Sophia Loren & Sarah Bernhardt—who had over 1000 lovers & said, "it is by spending oneself that one becomes rich." This summed up the philosophy that drove Renee. Bernhardt also slept in a coffin lined with love letters. If Renee wanted to go with one of her faves, contrary to my druthers, I'd go with it. & whatever she cost I never blinked 'cause I never got short-changed. Most ordinary dames don't have to cost you an arm or a lifetime. If you know how to shop around, you can spot "IT" (the opposite of the Louise Brooks kind of "it"). The ones that'll hang from your balls, ring'm like church bells till you cough up a collection box full o' green. Terrain, snuffed hopes, diets, sex satisfaction, & greed all mark up a face in one way or another.

I used to go mainly for the lonely *bell du jure* [*sic*] kind. They don't bitch & aren't all stuck on vainity [*sic*] & bored getting into the ooomph of things. & they're always busy making up for lost time. & they talk it up to drown out the grunts of ecstasy, telling you why they need your green: ballet lessons for Lisa; spending cash while hubby camps in the slammer.

On top of that, any hooker left of Lassie is going to sap you like a maple. Lead you on like a peep show. Killing any feelings to just go on living. But, by then, why bother?!

On the other hand, Renee wings right into your life like a swarthy flamenco, like a sultry satellite spinning on its slender axis. Yea, stuff gets through despite the mask.

She's a one-woman show. Costumes accurate to the stitch. Elaborate sets. Meticulous attention paid to scent, nuance, body language, accents & attitude. She puts you in pictures, but she's not afraid to fudge her lines to point out some abuse meted out by Hollywood against its starlets. Or to avenge casting couch ghosts. How quickly Francis Farmer & Gene Tierney are forgotten, she seems to be saying.

But she's also been Mamie Van Doren as the provocative mom in *High School Confidential*, & Nastassia Kinski as *Tess* taking the luscious yearning-drenched strawberry in her mouth. Her repertoire is wide open.

I could have Divine if I wanted, but I don't. Others do though! Or Eva Braun! Hitler's blond bundle, complete with swastikas & leather knee-high boots. Or Betty Boop. Or Darla Hood, darling "Little Rascals" heartthrob. Yea, I got all done up as Alfalfa once, in overalls, freckles, & cowlick, yodeling for my Darla. It was OK. Goofy, but OK.

But Renee plays the jailbait trip real cool & discreet. She doesn't deny the potential for arousal. But she has to avoid dangerous compromises of herself & a possible vice squad visit. She issues a disclaimer & post-performance lecture on child porn. She clarifies that it's OK to FANTASIZE that she, Renee, is 12. But she insists on being the screen for the cinematic projections of nubile obsessions. In other words, she has to channel aggressions, collar fantasies that are biting at the bit to go ape. But sometimes things go wrong.

Not long ago, a dazed & repressed evangelical minister beat her up bad. She played Brooke Shields straight out of *Pretty Baby* & he played George C. Scott in *Hardcore,* his mirror ego of a hardass dad whose daughter gets sucked up into a runaway porn whirlpool. He got his kicks hating the very accuracy of Renee's portrait. Renee's take on this holy hooligan is that he wanted to punish Brooke through Renee, as well as punish himself for his own hypocrisy in coming to Renee in the first place!

Life's not easy & so Renee has not only to be Brooke but to play priest, bouncer & social worker as well. In this case she got a black eye, bruised ribs, & a shredded costume. (He ripped it off of her with his chompers! & then stiffed her for $200!) So wow, for sure she has herself some hidden knives. Knows Tai Kwan Do.

But who IS Renee? The sum of her costumes, sequines, laughs, wigs & the masks she makes herself?

The process of making the masks, fascinating in itself, also sheds light on who she is. First, since most of her subjects are dead or otherwise inaccessible, she's had to scout out likenesses, busts, statues & wax museums. Then enamor herself to the proprietors to allow her to make the necessary moulage plaster cast of the subject, from which she casts her polymer mask. The mask is made of a skin thin latex ultra-polymer, like rubber, thin as a condom or coat of paint. Recently she's regained her confidence in sculpture so now she sculpts most of the subjects first, then dips the bust in the ultra-polymer.

Why the masks? Well, she used to be a known summer stock actress, an Off-Off-Broadway director, costume designer, puppeteer, & sculptress.

The best I can piece her together is that she had a face that could make even the gift of her body (Hindu goddess curvacious) jealous. Like Grace Kelly. A face photographers might duel to the death over. Photos in her Yale yearbook & in old theatre programs bare [*sic*] this out. Her face popped out of any crowd like a silver dollar in a pile of pennies.

She'd played Cherry Lane & La Mama in New York as well as some bit work in soaps, Provincetown & Woodstock. She's done Shakespeare, Ionesco, & Tennessee Williams. Which means something to others but not that much to me.

She said I'd like Tennessee 'cause he does alot about drunks falling apart & weird sexual stuff. She recommended "Sometime One Summer," where a guy parades his sis around as sex bait for neighborhood guys. She told me about this 10 years ago. Holy Christ! I really should check them out—for HER sake at least. But bookstores smell like funeral parlors to me.

But why with the masks? Well, now & again we'd belt back a few gimlets, grasshoppers, mint juleps—whatever was appropriate to the chosen fantasy—& we'd get to talking. I never pried, mind you. Her parents, bitter aging "Mormon Monsters," told friends & relatives that they had had no kids! No daughter! She don't exist!

& the face? It had something to do with a motorcycle. A bit part won in the biker flick *Devil's Angels,* where she played the love distraction of John Cassavetes. At a cast party a hot dogging biker, exhilirated perhaps by the fact that she was on HIS bike with HER arms wrapped around HIS waist, hit a hole & she got thrown with her foot caught between the exhaust & frame. He dragged her a couple of hundred feet before he noticed. & by then her face was scraped off., leaving a crude erasure, a blank slate.

I didn't go into it. I've seen my share of dead truckers & highway hamburger. & by then she changed the subject because she didn't want to further "muck up the paid-in-full revved-up reveries that *must* sustain us."

Told me I was her fave. The only marriageable item around. If only marriage had been more becoming to her. & then there was the small detail of my wife. & it wasn't only 'cause I tipped big either, although a fat wallet that yaks she don't mind listening to. Maybe all this flattery produces more green. Who knows. But I believe her—

even with an Anita Ekberg accent. Even if she says I remind her of Monty Clift. & Victor Mature the next time. I been called worse [*sic*].

I wasn't into the knockers stuff much. Anymore than a handful is wasted anyway. (Renee's are like sun-ripened bartlets.) The bushel basket racks of Jayne Mansfield mostly leave me queasy, like a kid with too much candy. Unreal maumaus make things too cartoony, too much like bad architecture—a parody of desire.

I *did* go in for her Lilly Christine, legendary "Cat Girl" stripper. How'd she know I'd seen Lilly (had I mentioned it, was she psychic?) when as a mere sprout my ole man'd drag me around to smokey joints? I remember the damp arcs of perspiration under rotund men's arms, the hearty laughter, the click of billiard balls, clank of glasses, the strip joints with exotic feathers, & an avalanche of raunchy colors.

& here I was living the rewritten deja view [*sic*] dream of actual experience. Not only did Renee get the tits right but she came alive as the sh-boom shimmering perfection of a smoldering ember fabrication during her undulating re-creation of Lilly's "Pillow of Love" dance; during which she hangs various boudoir articles on my ears, nose, fingers & erection. Then wraps her blond tresses around my face as the canned boogaloo music that Lilli herself played percussion on, goes up tempo—savage.

I can smell her perspiration mixed with the glue that holds her fish-scale pasties in place. Every tantalizing gyration provokes my pulse & my pulse in turn urges her gyrations on, which in turn shove the music along until her sequined gyrations are just this boundless blur, this comet of climax & joy. & when the music finally dies I am dead. I am spent, whittled down to an out-of-breath, pimply, gawky 13 year-old.

She wraps her arm around me & leads me with a purr to her "UNdressing Room." Implores me there, as footman, to remove her shimmering stilletos. Commands me to kiss the crenulations caused by the tight straps across the bridge of her foot. Her entire body aglow, pulsating, I help her from her sequined top with its huge secret diamond clasp. She shimmies out of her fish scale skimpy.

"Thank you, son," said my Blond Venus in all her naked splendor. "Lemme give you something for your trouble. My famous autograph perhaps?" Hmmm! Wink Wink. Act III.

For the longest time I would not play Sonny Bono to her Cher. Until she described HER brand of Cher one day: "A hippie-Indian princess with notions of being a svelte quasi-anorexic Theda Bera wearing her dazzling Mesopotamian-Dominatrix & Academy Award-attending homage to Rambova (first celluloid slut) & pre-psychedelic Busby Berkley."

She'd play her role as the goddess of OOmphalos [*sic*] with a winking jewel of fantastic cut in her most erotic orifice—her belly button. Wear a headdress of sumptuous porcupine at home, to lure Sonny away from his songwriting & moustache twirling. & in she bursts with her tanned bare midriff, "I'm home, honey! Come groom me!" & a moment later I'm her Sonny.

I never bothered to enter the "revolutionary mitsth" [*sic*] of Patti Hearst (long ago deleted), with her tied up in a broom closet mumbling her revolutionary rhetoric. No licking the white thigh-high boots of Nancy Sinatra. No Anita Bryant. No Mary Lou Retton leap-frogging furniture—too hyper. No Annie Oakley decked in suede fringe. No Joanie Weston, blond bone-crushing roller derby madame. No Astrud Gilberto, fronting a jazz combo, all sultry & blasé in Ipanema micro-kini.

I went mostly where she went—quality. It hums longer. The images linger. Women of depth with some surface noise. Smoke & rumination. Being & always threatening to do. Bardot, Seberg, Gene Tierney, Garbo, Peggy Lee. Women—not dames, broads or girls. Women who read books & swing a mean barbed tongue. Women like a thick diary with a strong perfect binding, full of references, arrows, circled passages. Someone to read & re-read.

I've seen Renee 200 times. I've gone hundreds of miles out of my way to see her. Hey, but I'm not desperate. A trucker just gets to dreaming out there & Renee draws me into my reveries & that is good. & what, you may ask, do I give her? Well, money. Lots of it. But alot more. I mean, I get *into* my part, I get involved. & she says she can talk to me. Tells me things she's *never* told anybody! I don't know what it is (my face?) but women are always spilling their guts, their deep stuff. Maybe it was just a line. But with her I believed it.

Renee was not launched by notions of mansions & Mercedes (in tax land, discretion is the better part of intelligence), but more by romantic notions of affecting change—dismantling harmful myths about woman—in the collective unconscious of the man-dick.

Fruit fell from her Brazilian straw hat, rolled around her feet. She wrapped her giddy bod in satin theatre curtain, posed like Gypsy Rose Lee, taunting me way out of myself, shivering out of 100 skins, nude to the bone, discovering the skeleton that holds me up.

She taunts me with the red curtain like a torreador. Says I'm a bull. So I am. I lunge. She sidesteps me. The bull's neck muscles are severed just before it enters the ring. This drops the bull's head down so that the horns are more menacingly aimed at the bullfighter.

& here, on my knees, life seemed to reverberate beyond time. Belief, so rich in texture that life again began to feel warm, actually *real*, as if all its confusion was meant to be *lived* as a scene, a play within a play.

Then she pops her marionette trick. Pickle tied to strings between her legs, so that by tugging the strings the pickle looks like some martian boner. You had to be there.

& as she strips away the last gooey rags, the mother of pearl halter with the 2 limpet shells covering her nipples, she lectures me on how skin & political consciousness converge. Gypsy Rose Lee stripped for the Nationalist cause, donating the proceeds to the Anti-Fascists in 30s Spain. What realm of higher power was I in anyhow? Renee hovering between smoldering body aesthetic & formidable personality, endowed with history making her dangerous like the Maja Nude with boxing gloves.

When I got involved with her Gene Tierney in Shanghai I wanted it to go on & on. Haul around in a rickshaw. Take her to bars. Float around in junk. Meditate on Tierney's face, a face that humbled crystal, mugged you of your breath & yet hid a life of real emotional turmoil. Her trance-like gaze—as if confused by the idea that SHE might be god—broken only by twitchy hints of madness, a shivering lip.

Then one day I get an idea. When you haul cross country you get a lot of ideas. The more god-forsaken desolate the land, the more ideas. Thought I'd surprise her with some flowers. Skip the usual call. But this aint advisable with a control freak. You might's well haul off & hit her.

She didn't know I was there, sort of just hanging in a corner. & I overheard her with another guy. I'm not a particuliarly [*sic*] jealous guy, seeing as reality has imposed this provisionary give & take attitude on life. But what she was dishing was more than I could swallow.

She was drunk. OK. I'll give her that. Here she was dishing this guy the same lines. Same lines, just another leading man. & I have to sit there, ass on my hands. Maybe she's rehearsing for me. Maybe biz is biz & flattery makes all wallets flap wider.

I spot him leaving in a featureless new Ford. Government plates. I feel like Stanley Kowalski. I could punch a lampshade. When I confront her she's no one, not herself, no one I've ever encountered before.

She's supposed to be Ann Margaret. I can't talk to Ann Friggin' Margaret! I drop the flowers at her feet.

"I feel like Stanley Kowalski."

"Gonna be a rough night."

"& I know my GODDAMN lines—STELLA!"

"Something's wrong. What's with the flowers at my feet?"

"Nothin'. Nothin's wrong. 'Cept me. The world just sucks the big one sometimes."

"Somethin' happen? A check bounce?"

"How'm I different, Renee? What really makes me any different? Like from all the others."

"You're my man, my main guy. Special!"

"HUH! Aint that somethin' just like the line you dropped on Mr. Threads?"

"Oh, I get it. Snoopin'."

"Well, the volume was turned way up. Never mind the heat."

"So my acting's so effective you can't even tell a line from the real thing? That's a compliment, but I'm afraid I don't feel very complimented."

"That's right. My mind's been twisted around so many times I don't know when real's real no more. I know like acting is your reality & your reality is like not to have the 2 separated. You, you're livin' in a blender."

"The guy's dyin' for Pete's sake!"

"Aint we all."

"No, for real. Real soon. The guy paid up good. He was beggin'. Abandoned by his family & friends. Least I could do for an atheist, I'm closest to a priest for him, before he's sent afloatin' to oblivion."

"Don't go gettin' flakey poetic on me. What is it? Syph?"

"Cancer."

"Whatta you handin' me bullshit in gift wrap? I don't know anymore what to believe."

"Well, you don't own me."

"Write me another song that's already been written."

"If we were to get married..."

"We might's well be. I seen more o' you than my ole lady..."

"I'm jus' more memorable 's all. Anyway, he paid well & in cash for the lies to sound real."

"Got me there. They sounded REAL alright."

"Lemme get the script. I was Cleopatra."

"Ann Margaret as Cleopatra? Tha's a good one."

"& he's a warrior, Ben Hur-type, like Victor Mature."

"Victor Mature?! HUH! He looked more like Dennis The Menace's ole man! I'm your Victor, remember?"

"He's been tossed to the lions. But the script has me fallin' for him. I risk the throne by commuting his sentence."

"Wow. That's hard to swallow."

"Try. Heaven's nothin' more'n the way religion candycoats the bitter pill. It's interior decoration."

"So you're his religion?"

"Yea. & you, you're the reality barometer?"

"Don't go mistakin' whorin' for evangelical faith healin'. I mean, lay your hand on me Renee, Baby."

"OK, so chop me down to 2-bit entrepeneur, & you be just a consumer lookin' for his bargains. We can work it out. Next time you get me cheap. & I'll break. You play with me too much."

By then I've had enough. I plunge through the rickety screen door, make as if to storm off—forever.

"Renee, you's the one always tellin' me actin' aint lyin'."

"It aint. & consoling aint lyin' either."

I couldn't take it. I always storm off when there's no winning. I considered torching her chicken shack. & in my haste left behind my last script scribbled on the back of one of Lucky's menus. I don't recommend the clam chowder. Unless you like already-been-chewed gum.

You're Maria Schneider playing Jeanne, wayward girl disillusioned by her cinematically-distracted boyfriend who wants to make a movie of her life to prove his love. & I'm Paul, ex-boxer, strung out on grief. He's struck by Jeanne. So much so he eliminates all manners to get to the soul of living.

> *Jeanne: "Ooh, what strong arms you have."*
> *Paul: "The better to squeeze the fart out of you."*

Jeanne: "& what long nails you have."
Paul: "The better to scratch your ass with..."

For the next 8 months I went out of my way to actually avoid her shack. Was gonna let her stew. But then I got this haul to Couer d'Alene in Potatoland, home to a bunch of numbnut Nazis, only 4 hours from her shack. So I don't know whether it was foregiveness or horniness—let's just say my pretention to pride collapsed—but I paid her a visit. What'm I supposed to do? Cut off my dick to spite my wife, er my life?"

So I pull up in the dusty lot. On her screen door, a sign: BACK IN 10 MINUTES. I could wait 10 years but I smell she aint coming back no time soon. So I head to Lucky's. The tired-skinned sullen waitress who's never even attempted a smile in her life, smiles (like others spit) when I ask her the scoop.

"You didn' hear?"

"Would I be askin'?"

"She's taken up ill."

"Wha's THAT mean?"

"She took some punches. Some crazy flipped on her..."

"Ah, fuck! Where's she at?"

"Bozeman General."

I tended to blame myself. Like in a film where we think we can have impact. Where we can make things happen, as opposed to things making us happen. Anyway, Bozeman: blue skies, everything crisp, clear cut. Like hope was a gutted fish. A hush. Traffic is in no hurry to go nowhere. Beautiful old movie marquees hint at lost grandeur. They don't want to let me see her. I tell them I'm her brother—all that acting finally comes in handy. They believe me! She's wearing this gauze post-surgical mask.

"You look like Bogie's sister. 'Member *The Man Behind The Mask?*"

"John, I'm so..." The gauze mask billowing & collapsing with her every breath.

"Don't tell me. Another act. A new mask."

"I'm bein' held together by this thing. You know, like the skin around a tomato."

"Yea, like a tomato."

"Hazards of Academy Award acting no doubt." It took her awhile to spill the story. Voice slurred, flickering & hoarse, like a distant radio station. Throat had been cut!

"I didn't know the human body contained so much blood!" Her mouth wired up. Shot up with Novocaine. On Demerol. Each drowsy word like the jab of a dull knife.

"Pain reminds you that you aint dead yet. Funny."

"Well, I guess 'at's somethin'."

"Maybe it actually did my face some good. Maybe it put some things back where they belong."

The story was like some sleazy detective page turner. This guy had been a regular. Tense Calvinist banker. Always ordered up the same scene. Trying to out control a control freak. Needed every detail to be just like the last time. A real stickler.

He wanted Paul Newman as failed jock (closet homo—that's the irony! but we weren't laughing) Chance Wayne, & Renee played Geraldine Page's Alexandra Del Lago, withering alki starlet. Every drink, vase, every dusty strawflower, doily, ruffle, mannerism had to be just right. Even had to be posed like the last time. But Renee tired of this wasted scene of self-degradation & abuse & insisted he choose new scenarios. & that he did. With a vengence. The next time he chose Alex, main *Clockwork Orange* droog. & she's the writer's wife brutally raped & eventually killed by Alex & his hooligan droogs.

This she didn't mind. She always insisted on certain parameters requiring certain simulations when foreign objects were introduced,

& she'd dealt with abuse & rape before. She counseled her clients, insisting on the non-sexual aspects of rape. But he seemed immune to these parameters. A vicious spoiled preppie who'd learned that all of life had its price. Seemed to enjoy trashing her. Not enjoy perhaps, so much as find unbearably necessary. As if he were "free" for the first time in his life. Like a brat vandalizing his first cemetery. She had to cut the session short. Told him to not come back unless he changed his attitude.

The *next* time, she said, he chose the corrupt, crazed sheriff to her Yvette Mimieux in *Jackson County Jail.* Where she's wrongly incarcerated & eventually preyed upon. Is brutally beaten & raped.

Renee figured this as the challenge of her life, & in true altruisitic fashion took his bullshit by the stink & wanted to set this guy straight or send him rolling. If not by counseling then by radical surgery—like castration.

But the scene came unravelled. He fell out of character. & when a character fell out & away she'd lose all directorial control, & a scenario quickly became a crime. He'd jumped far out of character & into something far more gruesome, out of illusion, out of play, out of his 3-piece suit, his prim lifestyle, out of protocol, wife & coif, out of all social dimension.

He'd reached for her face, yanked away her mask, & was so horrified by her disfigurement & the betrayal of the illusion of beauty that he flipped & began to bludgeon her with his shoes—expensive Guccis, too expensive to be wasting on her face.

"Sometimes my duty should be more to myself & not to the adventure of what I think is myself. Not always go around soothing the savage beast inside man. But sometimes someone's gotta do it or this planet'll be in even more trouble than it already is."

"Yea, OK, OK. Just get better."

"What's better?"

"Don't know."

"I feel like Vincent Price when his partner torches his House of Wax & he's forced to witness his precious Joan of Arc melt before his eyes. You know, John. I once killed someone. A customer. As Theda Bera. 10 years ago."

"You told me that one before.'Theda Bera, vamp with bonecrusher hips who handled snakes, slept in a coffin with skeletons.'"

"It's true. All of it. Me &—or her. I had to drop Theda from the menu."

"I thought, I don't know, it was just you being in character trying to shock me."

"This guy made a grab for Theda's hair. Yanked me 'round the set. Used me as a broom. I was doin' some coke back then. Whatever came my way. But it's true. I killed him in a fit of clarity with my suit of armor. Bludgeoned him unconscious. Didn't stop there. I was beside myself. Someone else."

"Yea, yea. You kept him in a closet for weeks until one night you buried him out on the mesa. Right?"

"No, not exactly."

"So when's the truth true for you?"

"When truth serves a purpose. I mean, I embroidered it for you. Actually, I dragged him out to Lucky's incinerator. Eh, you know the goon you caught me with?"

"Dennis The Menace's ole man."

"Yea, well, he aint no ordinary customer either. He's a tax man. IRS. He knows my story. So he's extorting hush money. Shakin' me down. For him to keep his flytrap shut I've got to pay *him* for *me* to service *his* fantasies."

"Like mob stuff."

"Exactly. He knows the inside dope. He knows I'm a small nation, a little outlaw island unto myself. He even seems to be onto rumors of the 'unfortunate & untimely passing away,' as he puts it, of a business associate of his."

"The guy in the incinerator?

"Yea." & then suddenly she shifted gears. Went into overdrive. Was her old self—or herself—without-self again.

"Oh, so what's *this* for?"

I didn't get her question. I mean I'm no improv whizz.

"Remember? *Ooh what strong arms you have?*"

"Yea, yea." I was amazed she'd kept that script inside her.

"*All the better to squeeze the fart outa you.*"

"*& what's this for?*"

"*That's your happiness & my ha-penis...can I open* (indicating her gown) *that? Hmmm. Wait a minute, maybe there's jewels in it. Maybe it's gold. You afraid?*"

"No." She tried. I couldn't go on. I was crying. For the first time in years. Crying at the feebleness of this stab at dignity. Crying because in my brain I was already re-writing Hitchcock's *Rope*."

"It's like I got hamburger make-up. The latest foundation—Steak Tartare!" she joked.

Or maybe I could improve on *Compulsion* with Orson Welles, improve on that "perfect crime." Or re-read Dostoyevski's *Crime & Punishment*. Re-read Chandler. Hammett. Yea, I've read those guys. But I need to re-read them. Do it right. & for real. Be the lead, the director, co-producer & co-conspirator.

"Brigitte Bardot supposedly once got a lawyer to lower his fees by lifting her skirt in his office. She said, 'In love is my only profession. My lover is the center of my existence. My limbs & thoughts cling to him.' I didn't say it, *she* did!" Renee went on. She was somewhere else. I had no idea where my own mind was at.

"I'm thinkin', Renee, when's Dennis The Menace due back?"

The text continues on at this point but only in the diary of Big (& dare I say "Bad") John. Or, perhaps too, in the police blotter of some western Montana town, as a crime stat. & every time someone is executed anywhere in the states—it's silly, but—I read the articles, hold my breath, looking for his name. My apologies Big John. You're an amazing guy & I deeply regret if my indiscretion here causes you any grief or legal difficulties. ▼

THE BEER MYSTIC'S CONTEMPORARY COCKTAILS

(FOR THE LONG HOT SUMMER OF OUR LACK OF CONTENT)

David Borchart

> *When I have 1 martini I feel bigger, wiser, taller. When I have a second I feel superlative.*
> **• William Faulkner**

1. THE JERSEY SUNRISE

4 oz. Hi-C® (10% real fruit juices)4 oz. lo-cost rum 2 oz. Carnation® Instant Breakfast (strawberry flavor)
1 oz. Pepto-Bismol®
• Mix in blender. Pour over Secaucus tap water ice cubes & into lipstick-stained 16 oz. styrofoam cup.

2. THE JERSEY SUNSET

3 oz. Wine Cooler®
3 oz. Yoo Hoo®
4 oz. peach brandy
• Add Yoo Hoo® to Wine Cooler® in unrinsed Johnson & Johnson beaker. Then gently pour peach brandy down side of beaker. When brandy has sunken gelatinously to bottom, drink up with breathless gusto!
• For a truly sinister topographic treat; pour "Sunset" over 2 pink Hostess Snoballs®. Let soak for 1 hour - & voila! - "The Jersey Speed Bump," our very own version of the exquisite "Baba Rhum."

3. HOOKER HYGIENE

6 oz. Bols® Creme de Banana
3 oz. White creme de menthe
4 oz. Nite Train Express®
2 oz. Schmirnoff® Vodka
2 oz. Cool Whip®
• Pour liquid ingredients into unused lambskin condom. Tie open end into knot. Drape liquid-filled condom over shoulder in manner of a goatherd's wine skin. Pinprick condom's reservoir tip. Drink cocktail in squirts as one would drink from a wine sack.

4. DAN QUAYLE 7&7 PARTY AGENDA (1996)

4 oz. 7Up®
4 oz. Diet 7Up®
2 oz. Diet Sprite®
1 packet of Pop Rocks®
1 packet of Punch Fizzies®
4 oz. St. Regis® (non-alcoholic) Champagne

• Mix liquid ingredients. Let sit until all latent "bad alcoholism-related" bubbles have been eliminated. Add Fizzies® & Pop Rocks® for wholesome bang. Sip with bewildered smile from a vintage McDonald's Desert Storm Series cup, happily deceived by cocktail's firepower.

5. THE UNCHAINED COED

2 oz. Leroux Peach Basket Brandy®
2 oz. Diet Mountain Dew®
2 oz. Cointreau® Licquer
2 drops of Opium® perfume
12 sweet Texas Honeydew melon balls
6 Supersoft Campfire® Marshmallows

• Pre-melt marshmallows. Mix with warm water. Pour into male/female genitalia-shaped ice cube trays. Pour well-stirred liquid mixture over genital cubes into long stemmed margarita glass. Add melon balls. Sip through coco-butter-greased curlicue glass straw. Exotic libertine!

6. **SLAMDANCE SKATEBOARD**

12 oz. Budweiser®
12 oz. Rolling Rock®
40 oz. Midnight Dragon Gold Reserve Ale®
40 oz. Silver Bullet®
12 oz. Black Label®
12 oz. Meister Brau®
32 oz. Colt 45 Malt Liquor®
24 packets of sugar (pilfered from local restaurant)

• Mix in vat (old oil drum). Let sit uncovered until all liquid ingredients are appropriately flat (all gases escaped). Dust lightly with cut Angel dust. Serve in water-proofed, well-worn Dr. Martin's boot. Sip, sneer, grumble menacingly & pass it around the circle jerk.

7. **THE ASCETIC**

2 oz. Perrier® Water
2 oz. Evian® Water
2 oz. Poland Springs® Water
2 oz. Badoit® Water
2 oz. Contrex® Water
2 oz. Volvic® Water
2 Local distilled tap water ice cubes (free of air bubbles, chemicals & im-purities.)

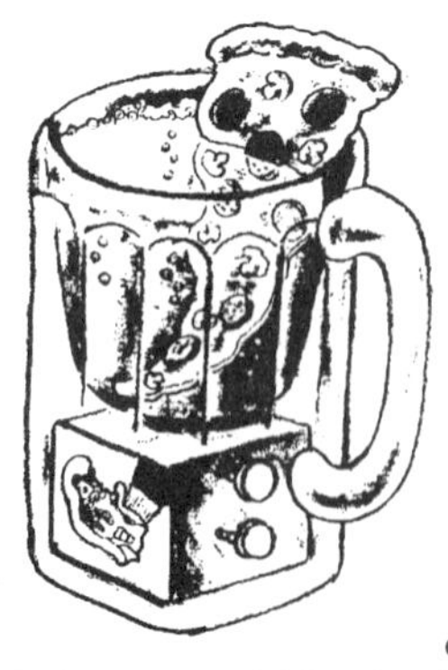

• Stir by hand for at least one hour until mix begins to hint at frothing. Serve lukewarm in any available glass to yourself, alone, in a dimly lit room, overlooking an airshaft or empty field with white noise on the radio.

8. SPAMFISTED STAIRMASTER

200g mega-anabolic androgen-based steroids
2 ultra-dessicated buffaio testicles
3 oz. sweat wrung from cut-sleeve Hard Rock Cafe® T-shirt
2 mega-raw turkey vulture eggs
6 oz. Dewar's White Label Scotch Whiskey®
2 oz. health spa mineral water

• Mix liquid ingredients in blender. Dissolve steroids in liquid mixture. Add buffalo testicles & vulture eggs. Liquify until frothy head forms. Pour into heavy dumbell-weighted mugs. For extra manly touch, stir cocktail with beef jerky stick. Guarantee: No earthling will doubt your gender with this concoction in your fist.

9. THE HEGEMONY FROO FROO DELITE

1 oz. testosterone
1 oz. Absinthe (or 2 oz Pastis OK)
2 oz. Absolut Scandinavian vodka
2 oz. fresh blood (beef blood OK)
4 oz. generic East European Vodka
4 oz. generic Puerto Rican slum Rum
6 oz. Evian® Water
2 NoDoz pills
2 Excedrin® tablets (generic aspirin OK in a pinch)
1 Tylenol II® capsule
2 packets Sweet & Low (or saccharine-based artificial sweetner)

• Dissolve tablets & capsules in liquid ingredients. Shake vigorously until frothy. Serve in mock eucharistic chalice. A special concoction for those who need to quaf & get coiffed before crawling fashionably disheveled up out of the pinched nerve of bohemia & into the parking garage, cranking up the grunge muzak in the Saab.

10. THE AMOUREXIC

2 tablets ExLax®

4 oz. bee pollen-oyster enema formula

l oz. annitol (baby laxative)

6 oz. SlimFast® "Tropicoco" Shake

4 oz. Amaretto liquer

2 oz. Hi-fibre bran

•Stir ingredients. Pour into enema bag. Moisten end of tube with fruit rind & dash of Angostura bitters. Serve orally or rectally.

11. THE WHITE TRASH BUNGEE JUMPER

2 oz. Herb-Ox® chicken flavor bouillon

1 oz. A-1 Steak Sauce®

3 oz. peppermint schnapps

3 oz. banana liqueur

3 oz. blue curaçao

3 oz. Southern Comfort®

2 oz. Mylanta®

2 Kraft Fat Free SmartBeat American Flavor Nonfat Slices®

2 cocktail cherries

2 pickled onions

• Pour into 2 Lynnrd Skynnrd Memorial cups over cracked ice. Stir with 2 Jimmy Dean Flapsticks® (fluffy pancakes, hint of syrup wrapped around Jimmy Dean sausage on a stick). Top with a colorful holiday rooftop (reminiscent of X-mas decorations) of Kraft slices, cherries & pickled onions. Pop in any video with more than 30 min. of chase scenes or 30 buckets of spilled blood. Sit back on plaid glider couch. Await your special oblivion. (Effective as a sledgehammer or broken bungi cord.) ▼

ERECTION SET

Kaz

I play golf, I'm a member of the Rotary Club & sometimes I like to have a young lady hang heavy objects off the head of my penis.
• R.J., letter in *Triple XXX Letters*

He still had the photo (sepia discolor like an old painting with too much varnish): him in cowboy fringe holding his Erector Set fire engine like a trophy. Like something he'd shot. He'd just showed them how the extensible ladder worked. Extending out. Rising up. The crank, the string, the pulley.

Where did it go? & that rattle of loose parts in a box? A sound he'd searched for in jazz & music from Brazil. A sound he'd thus far not found.

He had gone through an alphabet of women too. A passage of terror, delight & regret. None were ever to become the rattle in that box nor the photogenic trophy that could make pride leap from the confines of the snapshot.

But he was always capable of manufacturing the right pose for snapshots by the X-mas tree. He could squeeze her shoulders against his chest. He could flex to enlarge his sinking ship tattoo, or just hot dog it so that years later it would look like fun was had. Goose her into the ideal cheesecake pose. Hold a carving knife to her throat in sinister jest. & him posed there in his I-AM-HAPPY-PROUD-INVINCIBLE & crumbling stance. "Snap your snap," he'd say. "Let me find my beer," he'd say. "You should've initialed your cup," Dana would say.

Dana made love to him in the Denver Zoo. Often. She liked the African Savannah, where giraffes chewed sweet grasses & gazelles skitted past. She liked the adventure, the musky fragrance of rutting, pollen & field green clinging to the tips of their boots. But at the shivering convergence of grunt & moan, career & lifestyle, she giggled! The sudden stabs of ridicule are all we salvage of pride. This did not suit him.

At first he dug her zoo joke, her giggle, her mimicking the high-pitched grunts of giant gerbil-like mammals who ate cabbage, & dug up tubers & grub worms with their snouts at parties. The name of this peculiar mammal always eluded him. He asked friends. Went to the Bronx Zoo. He tried encyclopedias, & a peccary it wasn't. & an in-joke, a hug now & then & an orgasmic giggle in the zoo could not sustain a life, a life of voracious despair.

After the "accident" he began to see his injury as key to her freedom (he heard she eventually became a moto-cross champ), & fumbled with the hearsay that perhaps it had been no accident. That the "accident" had been eerily precise. Indeed.

When he first noticed Fossie she reminded him of a gushy Sophia Loren or what Loren'd look like had she, too, worked for 3 years in this lousy company cafeteria with hair balled-up under a hair net & a *Woman's Day* stuffed into a purse marked PURSE in big bold letters. Had he noticed her before? When she looked like someone else?

He liked her because she smelled of desperation. A geography of well-laid scents. A short wet skirt in a hailstorm. She smelled of someone who had cruised along on the hubris of youth & beauty. A woman who had for too long waited for too big a pay off. A finger-worn puzzle piece in search of a lost puzzle.

He was this company's quality control consultant. She knew that. He wore ties & he knew just how he wanted his lunches—no mayo, no Cremora. & this, she assumed, meant he was someone. Someone with a classy way out—or in.

He quickly learned to exploit her flaunted vulnerability & slight limp. Made a kind of samba out of it. This wasn't cruel, but playful. It made the lunch rush interesting. He ventured jokes about the so-called food. He salvaged ragged remnants of a former handsomeness, which he'd toss at her. He acted like he knew who he was supposed to be.

"How's yer thighs smothered in mushroom sauce, today?" Or "Are your grapefruits fresh & juicy?" He polished up clichés in that brash boyish manner & made them new. Amusing. Forgiveable. How they became so forgiveable remained a mystery, a mystery of

DNA unraveling like a party favor. She worked the register with long pink nails the way Van Cliburn worked a piano. Lovely to watch her fingers strike the keys: 5-2-3, 4-7-7-enter, 3-6-8, like numeric waltzes. She no longer worked the kitchen & so was no longer one of them, with their limp hair, sweating over vats of greasy steam. & one day something—happenstance?—made her long hair fall from its net.

Then one night in front of the blue comfort of the TV she took in her uniform so that her voluptuousness could boast forth its vocabulary of gathered curvaciousness. Sexiness on the job, however, is seen as disruptive. Subversive even, as if aesthetics is the enemy of work, & her battles with company policymakers were epic, many & notorious.

He ventured to tickle her palm when he paid his check. Which reminded her of descriptions of states of grace she'd once read about. No love letter had ever spoken so profoundly, & she began to deduct desserts & more & more with each emboldenment. & the loose change—the 53 cents here or 47 cents there—he in turn insisted, was always hers. As he put it, "I only like neat round figures." The breath of his eyes dwelling on the respite of each word in the sentence. Eyes flickering up & down "the adventure of her rollicking coast."

"You should have enough for a round trip on Trailways to Scranton by now."

"Whatchu? A English Major?"

"Yea, uh no, but I got a thick thesaurus."

He played their first date cool. Caressed her fingers. Told her how each finger was a highway to a different organ, "& the middle finger, well, uh..." Complimented her cuticles. Did an outline of her hand on paper. Which he folded, put in his shirt pocket, close to his heart. Which convinced her he was not like other guys. He did not possess the typical beer-fueled battering ram brain.

Called the next day to tell her about a dream: A rain of Autumn leaves all in the shape of her traced hand.

Second date: the second bottle of Spanish sherry impelled his pelvis into her hip. He sawed away on her jutting bone in the bath of the TV light, as if scratching a deep deep itch he couldn't quite reach.

One ready hand flexed the hidden atomizer as he smothered her with the sauce of misshapen swooning. Surveyed the contours of her luscious "lambscape." Marked the boundaries of her soul with hickeys & moans.

"It's like you're worming your way back into the womb," she remarked.

His hand functioned as sextant. His need (to satisfy her) served as pole star. His every command became her equilibrium. Drudgery became navigable. Lust got confused for vision, the way a cloud bank looked like land to conquistadors.

During a chase scene through sienna western dust she bounded from glider couch to "saddle," gripping emerging rolls of jellybelly as reins. She ground her wishbone into pelvis as sherry dribbled from her smirk.

He was hard & proud as Roman statuary. Hard as a mugger's blade, like in the days before the "accident." & this hardness flattered her.

She purred, bit his nipples like he'd wanted her to. Made out the contours of his truncheon with her virtuoso digits. Yanked down his pants the way a scavenger skins its prey. She re-mounted him, hair a frazzled halo, hand gripping truncheon as pommel. & her knees grazed a clear vinyl belt.

She could not have noticed him fumbling with the rubber ball which sent a mist, a wet spray, through slender tubing. This gas-suspended fluid's precise formula of polycyclic alcohol, propylene glycol (used in hydraulic fluids), blood plasma, erythoxylin coca, enters the penis directly under the scrotum. Its function: to create a recognizable & realistic vaso-congestive erection.

The atomizer kit (unassembled) is a relatively cheap ($3,200), primitive, yet effective version of the microchip electro-chemical stimulator ($15,000 + cost of implantation).

His free hand, meanwhile, fondled her hypno-pendulous breasts until her nipples grew hard & solid as rubber sink stoppers. With her eyes closed, head dangling back, precariously free of all constraint—oomph oomph—she imagined a sculptor, maybe from France, maybe turn-of-the-century!

Her ululations, hoseannas of agonizing histrionic pleasure with deep eerie gutteral moans full of shards of mucous, sounded like a girl scout with her flint rock striking rock, cracking off fat wet sparks. Eyes rolled up, a window shade revealing a 3rd eye mid-forehead.

All this drove him crazy, the way the scent of gunpowder did. Like the first mile of free fall as an Army parachutist. He ripped her blouse open sending bone buttons across his chest & onto linoleum. This sent her heaves & bucks to ever greater altitudes & sent the glider couch careening across new latitudes. Her head heaved & finally crashed against the wall, knocking the belly dancer velvet painting to the floor.

He feigned smothering sounds as her breasts continued to flog his face. (Maybe the belt was a truss or had something to do with weight control or sexual enhancement? Or was it part of a colostomy bag contraption?) Her eyes grew big as a cat's at night. She churned her behind & switched on the butterfly flutter action (setting #4).

The rubber ball in his left hand, to a novice, would have looked like a raccoon's heart or a baby's bath toy.

"What's with the belt?"

"Money."

"& yer hand?"

"Lucky charm."

"Why d'yuh gotta squeeze it?"

"It's only lucky if you squeeze it. Shut the light!"

"Aye aye. Cap'n Crunch with his lucky charm."

He darted his tongue into the midst of her plump (3 catchers' mitts) behind as she reached for the light, which earned him a screech of her delight.

"What's that sound? You leave a blender on?" Now he was imagining things.

"Maybe the fridge. It's on its last legs. Relax!"

He stepped out of his boxers. Ears trained to the source of the odd sound. Cold floor seeped through sweaty socks.

& on the bed she kneeled deep in prayer. Her tongue poked into his urethric slit. The sensory tip of her pinkie caressed something, something...

"Kneel!"

"I yam, I yam already, Cap'n Crunch." Flabby behind—BaBOOM, BaBOOM—anticipating the flattery of his rigid penetration. Swish Swish Swish. Like the wink of a damp cyclopic eye.

He spit into the mitt of her behind & rubbed his truncheon there. He remembered Midwesterners buttering their corn: butter a slice of white bread, then ream the ear through the bread.

"What is that?"

"What's what?"

"That squishy sound." She wanted to know. Durable clear transfusion tubing rubbed up against her. At that she impetuously rolled over as if going for the escape, the 2 points, the Ah-HA! Reached down to seize hold of the dimensions of his mythic beast.

& amongst the pulsing cord-sized veins & penile contours she noticed something peculiar, wrong, amiss. On the right side of his groin hung a rectangular protrusion & then something like bird bone or knitting needle or...

But she said nothing & let the beg of her vertical sigh accept this strange—appliance(?). Desire superceding suspicion. Heart palpitations coursed from temple to toe. Although neither of them could put those eerie sounds totally out of mind—the swish, slurp, squeak. The sound of 2 marionettes in need of glistening lubricant.

He rolled off of her & fell into groggy slumber. As he snoozed she lifted the sheet. Fingered the rectangular protrusion & from there her fingers, those digits of many numeric waltzes, laid upon the semi-prosthetic flexi-brace made of pliant pseudo-flesh & whalebone. Like a splint. Or a piece from an old Erector Set: For ages 4 to forever.

Then her finger found the belt, led her eyes to the holster which held the rubber ball—his "lucky charm"—followed the arc of the slender tube which led from the rectangular box to underneath the scrotum. She couldn't believe her discovery & hoped it might just be some hypnagogic mirage. Thereafter she fell asleep with her head full of hope on his thigh.

She dreamt of the time her brother built a brontosaurus with his Erector Set. The motor, a tight pack of gears & wire wrapped around magnets, & strings along pulleys which moved hinged joints so that neck & head moved in a slithery pixilated manner.

Her brother chased her around the house with the dinosaur between his legs, growling the way he imagined a dinosaur might growl.

He awoke to urinate. He stood over her recumbent plenitude. Yanked a pink Krazi-Nail, which she'd left behind like a farmer's daughter might leave a hoe cleft into soil, from the fleshy small of his back. He placed the pink sliver in his pants pocket.

He noticed how gruesome middle-aged people look asleep. As if the face of sleep is a bewildered grimace. He removed the lampshade from her nightstand lamp. Held the lamp under the sheet, caressed her mysterious lengths & folds with the light. Not quite knowing where to place her—& her apparatus, this "flesh-colored smokeless ashtray, this beckoning urchin from the ocean floor, from the lost continent of Atlantis, a form of animal life not yet classified into his or any cramped solar system of beliefs."

He read the literature he found in her nightstand drawer. This "urchin" did exist—in the "*entres jambes* of over 5,000 U.S. & European women." The French company, Vaginot (rhymes with Maginot), had named it "*Le Fleur des Entre Jambes*" or "The Flower Between the Thighs." He discovered that this life-like replica vagina, with "petal-soft" labia majora, with electro-chemically-released vaseline-based, perfumed lubricant oozing from the recreated pores of the replica vaginal walls, with a switch & graduated dimmer, with electric pump that reproduces the slight undulating sucking action effect was reported to be (& he would write a letter to concur) quite pleasurable to the male.

She awoke & propped floral pillows against the wall. She confessed how she'd been a victim. How the man had carved out her vagina in a fit of jealousy. How jealousy evolved into temporary insanity during his trial. How the factory let him come back after he'd done his time. She showed him how, when she cupped the labia, Le Fleur did, indeed, as advertised, form a corolla of petals around her stamen, her very intact clitoris.

Although their relationship was never a botanica of bliss, they did manage to stay together for 12 years. The first sustained relationship he'd had since his "accident" when a jut of car steel had severed function from image. Dana had been driving. Driving like a crazy. Crazy as a fox. A crazy with compelling focus, & aim. Or so the "accident" could be painted, given the right "psychological palette."

& then Fossie died at age 56 of something simple, unpronounceable & undiagnosed. He rummaged through her dresser for answers to the exact circumstances of her victimization. He found bundles of letters wrapped in ribbon. Some bad Polaroids during her bouffant days, languishing on the hood of a Dodge Dart on Daytona Beach. He found a box of stones, screws, butterfly barrette, tie clips, the odd rings he'd given her, cufflinks, a tooth, some costume jewelry.

He added her pink Krazi-Nail. He shook the box, & the box shook him & suddenly the rattle of memorabilia against the box sides rendered him a 3rd person soul in a 1st person body. So he'd bring this box along to the Wood Bee Bar where he'd dance. Jameson & ginger ale (her drink) in one hand, taped jewelry box in the other, rattling it like some maraca full of bird bones, sea urchins, teeth & nuts, votives & cat-eye marbles, flower stems, Erector Set parts & a lipstick-stained Tareyton filter—the specific archaeological particles of memory & reverie. ▼

PSYCHO-GEO-CATO TRAVELS

Orange

The more we can squeeze out of nature by inventions & discoveries & improved organization of labor, the more uncertain our existence seems to be. It seems not we who lord it over things...but things which lord it over us.
• Bertolt Brecht

The catalogue: the gun the catalogue the gun the catalogue was of the typical mail order variety displaying mostly soft things of linen of cotton to cuddly roll around in lost & costly, smiling & foetal.[*This is NOT a short story, though things do happen or rather are posed to appear to have happened.*]

Page 34: A veritable lingerie "horn(y) of plenty" or "hornicopeia of delites." Sumptuous leering mannequins offer up the winking pose of themselves in a classical genre that pinions its wholesome lasciviousness somewhere between French postcard, Goya's *Maja Nude*, 60s Sears Catalogue & pastry shop window. One section, called *Lingerie de la Patisserie*, thematically connected our penchant to associate class with anything that sounds like it may have been dragged along the cellar floor of a brie factory. & concurrently breasts became sweets (so that women would remain edible) such as whipped cream, so the brassieres of varying cuppages were duly christened—*Creme Nocturne, Creme de Menthe, Café Creme, Creme de la Creme*. These bras astonish & recall (for males) those early pangs of emissions *par main*. Back when women were omni-available, pliant & compliant. Some of the models are cut off at the neck (their necks & heads will reappear again in the jewelry section) & knee, the way a T-bone steak or lamb chop is cut off from its sustenant source.

Page 86: We see neatly groomed models to fuck to shoot at or look at. They look like guns or bombers or neatly groomed models with piles of headshots in their garrets. They operate bright toys of hard plastic molded to look like guns or cars. Some of the toys talked back, others moved of their own accord.

Page 105: Tools. Black. Variable speed. Shaped to be held by men who had long struggled to overcome the disorder of their environments. Tools that cut through things we had never cut through

before. Tools that peeled & vibrated. Tools we didn't even know we needed.

Page 122: The boys wore garments with immense sprawling labels meant to advance a sense of menace. Or identity. Or identity as menace. The boys stretched defiant sneers across their faces. This was the image of Turf Builders, self-described mondo clothiers of the street craze. We had been taught to covet them as diamonds, snatch them as gold chains. & the accrued status seemed to make men of boys. Because not only were the boys proud, they were full of fear. Turf Builders had, indeed, ushered clothing into a new dimension of expression & adventure.

Page 137: A smiling model asserts a stance that deprives him of his person. He is held together not by his powers of reason nor his ability to dream but by the leather & the esteem its superior manufacture seemed to guarantee. A hidden melancholy mocks the virility of his body type. Was he carrying a black valise full of dead meat? Had he lost his motorcycle? Was he suddenly too old to rock & roll?

Page 143: Same model is shown here amiably accompanied by several stylishly underweight female models. Their bodies inspire the dreams of TV. Their tummies tight as a kid's Indian drum. The variety of color seems to beg us to believe that Spandex had already left them reasonably satisfied, because their smiles seemed professionally rendered as they strained adroitly inside harnesses of various configurations. Some recalled cobwebs, or devices used during "THE TIME OF THE WITCH HUNTS."

Page 174: Model of lithe figure posed with neck & wrists inserted into holes of an "*objet d'art*" crafted by real country artisans. The "*objet*" was never actually refered to as a pillory, & thus could have been something else. It supplies our need to feel like part of the notorious drama of a history that only occurs as we consume it in the comfort of our own abode-bunkers. Cleopatra as line of makeup, Napoleon as pastry, Poison as scent, Gun as source of music to our fear-rendered inner ears. Besides, the model's smile seemed to indicate all was well.

Page 208: The pet supplies section seemed to display many objects (grommeted, stone-studded pleather) that mirrored products that humans had long ago desired into necessity.

[*Disclaimer: This is NOT a short story & should not be judged as one.*]

Page 209: This suspicion was amply confirmed by the matching tinted pleather dog collars for both "dog & master." The item was understandably & clearly marked: "gag gift." Human breakfast cereal that resembles Puppy Chow is also clearly marked as "NEW! NUTRITIOUS GAG GIFT!"

Page 213: Various beauty enhancement devices: one stretched shoes, another claimed to resculpt the human body using vibrating heat-induction pads. Presented also were special hangers for special garments. A model in bright sportswear hung from it to illustrate the acclaimed strength of design. A variation of the same hanger was touted as a "perfect child maintenance device," but was more costly than a high resolution television.

Page 232: Precise digital computation instruments measured the trajectory of various expended bodily fluids. Fluids under pressure. Fluids chilled by resentment. Fluids overheated by frustration. Fluids boiling, percolating. Aptly labeled: "for the modern family."

Page 249: Various odor-sensitive & light sensory alarms had begun to appear among the various electronic trip devices that guaranteed a secure home. Several designs of sonic or toxic anti-personal dispensers meant to ward off intruders & discourage undesired street encounters were offered at resonable discounts. All had been "police tested" & approved by an official organization that seemed to have links with the Central Government.

Page 275: The smiling skull & crossbones design is a registered trademark & indicates the catalogue's special section: "Armed Responses To Perceived Threats." A section introduced in 1986; a section whose growth & profits had been totally unforeseen.

Page 276: Standard firearms (portable for picnics, include both car-mount & window-mount designs) came with designer bullets that, when discharged, would whistle a pleasant tune as their noses expanded to cause more effective harm.

Page 277: The cross-section tangle of bright wires, sensory gates & micro-chips, although very attractive, comprised the internal workings of the lawn & garden variety of landmine that would explode—via telecommand—if all instructions were followed & all precautions taken. Success would then be imminent, & success would look tragic. Perfect for those who need to verify & protect unspecific property lines. Also recommended by the APA & the PBA for the esteem-deprived (See "Hitler's Dog") who've been denied a credit card.

Page 279: The cyanide capsules, in a choice of 3 improved fla-

Page 281: A selection of video & K7 tapes by major image merchandisers reproduced futures that had already deprived consumers of their own imperfect dreams. The variety of choices was invigorating, if somewhat predictable: a. Disney; b. Playboy; c. Situation Comedy Households; d. Extinct Wildlife; e. Bacchanalian Idealism in the Rock Video; f. Sports Heroes Prior To Computer-Enhanced Imaging; g. Club Med Promotional Tour of the World's Most Luxurious Swimming Pools; h. New Age Industry Tour of Great Waterfalls of the 20th Century;

Page 282: i. The Vatican's Fur-lined Chastity Belt Collection; j. Russ Meyer Documentary on the Girl Scouts; k. Hungarian Curlian Photography Healing Techniques; l. Fruitbat Imagery in the Paintings of Norman Rockwell; m. *Mademoiselle*'s 50 All Time Top Beauty Tips & Weight Loss Hints; n. The Unexpurgated *Girl From U.N.C.L.E.*; o. Changing Attitudes Toward Clitorechtomies & Depilation in Moravia.

Page 291: Special section devoted to Vintage Ethno-Aryan Pridewear (some are genuine garments with real epaulets worn by actual Nazi officers. Enclosed PC brochure assures buyer that the Swastika is actually an Indian Hindu symbol of peace). Others are official Bavarian recreations of Battlewear as worn by SS Officers in the heat of battle. To assure their genuine nature the pieces & ensembles are all individually titled & "signed" by actual Nazi casualties. Extra care to detail includes accurate placing of shredded bullet holes & bomb shard rips. Perfect for history buffs & those who like to periodically take orders from (be "overrun" by) their significant other in uniform.

Bulk Mail Flier: During the Autumn Sales Extravaganza, an ad campaign (combining sinister hip & ironic phobic deshabille) premiered in fliers, in Times Square on billboards & kiosks portraying wide-eyed models gleefully holding shiny pistols (shiny enough to see one's own image in the barrel's reflection) to their temples. ▼

INTERNATIONAL PARTS 1 - 9

Yossarian

> ***How ridiculous is the week-old wreath! A ring around the rotting neck.***
> **• Su Byron, *Paris Notebooks***

ONE

The town was no longer quiet. Nor as set in its ways as it had once been. Not with the golf course near by, built mid-war by LaLoma Enterprises which specialized in converting battle terrain into courses. Bomb craters into sand-traps. I had had a hand in that. The kind of hand you periodically wish you could lop off.

[*& I'd played violin with the dull paring knife across the blue "strings" of my wrist. More mocking than threatening, granted. As if ridiculing my own self-aggrandizing bathos. All to the extreme consternation, however, of the employees in the Wing Fun Sweet Indochine resto with their glazed food a l'emporter. They prefered to mistake me for just another heroinmaniaque from the Belleville Quartier of Paris. Of this puerile gesture you made note. Of this I was quite aware as you continued to question me. & of my awareness you never caught on & this was your first mistake in your earnest post-graduate, headlong & flushed-cheek pursuit of the truth.*]

More European cars now cruising the boulevards with their calm impenetrable (bullet proof?) arrogance. & all the blond Asians hinted at a mongrel elegance that had never been fully aroused. Streets teemed with bikes. Bells the latest gadget everyone had to have. Bells made Market Square sound like a grove full of swallows. Huge murals advertising toaster ovens & curling irons attracted huddles of skinny gawkers. Women & boys squatted behind crates & sold Chinese smokes one by one. Faces underfed, souls overdrawn. They were known to eat vermin & anything that ate vermin. It was bleak, but bearable. No less no more than Toledo, say. The food unadorned & unpretentious. Beer neither cold nor warm.

I had some time to kill before the assigned "necessary deprivations," & around here, if you didn't kill time it ended up killing you. But in this heat you swim in the same sweat with madness. No one moved unnecessarily. Everyone had a remedy for these *moustiques*, carniverous no-see-ums, a variety of gnat that gets particularly agitated when there's a storm brewing—or a battle. The bartender suggested cutting down on salt.

In this kind of nagging squalor you begin to hatch morbid entertainments. Like yanking the wings off flies. I pulled a fist full of clink & silver from my pocket, currencies from 6 nations. With a sinister desire to break the too quiet quiet I began to flip coins onto the sticky floor of the Lucky Bar, *the* place to buy Purple Hearts, chevrons, tags, passports & assorted booty stripped from "bloated floaties" found belly-up in the paddies.

In a deliberate tongue I said, "Only dolls," I sculpted a pair of tits in the turgid atmos, "who strip." [*I stood up for you also & sculpted much the same pair of breasts, but had your breasts as much in mind as the Indochine doll's. & with this gesture I was perhaps too subtle.*] Some smirked. Habitués kept the stone on their faces. One woman shaped like a wash basin finally went for the bait & stripped when she saw 3 months pay at her feet. Soon a dozen diminutive nudes with attractive low centers of gravity joined her. I added some crinkled Lincolns to augment the insanity.

The locals kept the stones on their faces, as we say. It was their country again but still not quite their place to speak. Some white men in blue—non-coms—laughed. They're the type to laugh when any woman other than their own wives is humiliated. The Lucky isn't the only bar I've ever been in that honored cowards.

A duet of the more intrepid dolls forewent the clink & silver & went right for me—the bank. They offered a wide range of services, everything from ironing to fellatio, in cracks of awkward English. Voices reminiscent of untuned string instruments. One cupped her coffee-stained breasts. Served them up like *Petite Religeuses*. & then she wrapped around me like a snake on fire, hair, eyebrows & pubis dyed pumpkin.

It was at that moment, in the blur of desperate niceties, in this topog of smoldering yellow craters, charred brittle forests, with her fingers (nails I wanted to clean with my teeth) wrapped around my knee, her body punched up with party bens & a lurid legacy of delirium tech, that I began to suddenly dream again. Derelict & flailing imagery at first. Stuff veritably bursting at the seams of logic. This then, was the debut of my 6th sense in a 4th world.

Eventually this 6th sense was infiltrated by some of the more uncalled for "life deprivations." I remembered the 3 Sisters of The Habit, the ones I'd watch, sleeves rolled, habits hiked, skimming the murky river for eels & carp. I remember the golden carp. The pride on their faces. The barefoot kids telling them it meant good luck. & then they became just 3 more of the 160,000 CIA "population control neutralizations." I remember the Steyr-II sniper rifle with its 26" synthstock barrel, & how the sniper talked to it like it was his pet dog.

I remember each crashing second of their deaths. It's now been 10 years since I've used synaptical blocking drugs & I've been dreaming ever since—often about the 3 Sisters. The past is still being scooped out of me with rusty hacking tools. & the agony comes by later to pick the bones clean.

& sleep—when it came at all—could only be defined as fitful twitches in a greasy patch of exhaustion.

TWO

I'd grown up polite. My window overlooked well-watered lawns. Basketball nets hung over driveways. In my room I plotted Napoleonic battles, & equally, revenge on girls who'd snubbed my advances. [*By this time we'd moved to a café down the hill, near where the Boulevard meets the Rue de Belleville. Here you shook your head in affirmation, offering some enthusiastic details to prove that you too had come from the horrible Mid-West, & you were with me & no longer so impartial.*] My skin was greasy, hair thin. Pants never fit quite right. To clothing manufacturers my shape just didn't exist. My girl was serious & unexceptional—like me. I remember someone (in my dorm?) refering to her as a cold water faucet.

In college I responded to an ad for the CIA. The motives: a dare & perhaps a bit of revenge. Besides, the CIA promised Challenge,

Responsibility, Diversity—CAREERS with new horizons...asssignments in foreign lands...the unusual personal & professional satisfaction that comes from a real contribution to your nation's security... [*You took note, had me repeat this slowly because you wanted each word of this to be exact. & this brought a bemused smirk to my face, which flattered more than flustered you.*] Needless to say, I had always taken the proper folding of our flag seriously. Couple that with the notion of needing to appear exceptional at something as a form of revenge on my peers & you have the profile of a candidate.

& in the course of my contributions to America's Security I was deprived of any bothersome moral compass I may formerly have possessed. What had been good & bad became necessary & unnecessary. I knew only the utility of compassion. In other words, a rat's best friend, if need be.

In that I'm NOT unusual, nor clean as a choir boy with a flag-pin. That I could easily become hero were the right target to face me, that my attraction to the job was not without competition & not without precedent & not without a future & not without a perceived *raison d'être* & not without a crowded field of wannabees is really the strange & ghastly side of all of us. I found reasons, steeped in all the facetious terms of lofty ideals, to outfit me. & this'd nauseate me if it hadn't already excited me so much. It's not at all that I LOVED targeting specified obstructions, no, just as a vampire bat doesn't LOVE seeking warm blood. He just does it. He & I had no choice. & I wasn't so much a main character as something in the stage's set, something wafting about in the air, a moan, a foul odor. That's me.

I began my career by authoring simple "multiple untruth" stories released to the local press. My most famous: WAR PAINT TRIBESMEN AMBUSH U.S. TOURISTS...WILD SPEAR-HEAVING NATIVES SMASH WINDOWS IN JUNGLE ATTACK...10 AMERICANS SUFFERED INJURIES...THIS IS NOT AN ISOLATED INCIDENT...STEPPED UP HOSTILITIES...ON U.S. TARGETS...COULD SERIOUSLY AFFECT TOURISM...

I bribed local politicos, propped up regional influentials, arranged drug frame-ups, deportations & fomented dissent so that natives (usually led by West Point-trained operatives) would eventually terminate a visible occidental. This was then escalated into "threats against U.S. business interests" which provided the impetus for the RDM (Rapid Deployment Marines) to perform their signature "stabilization maneuvers"—offense in the guise of defense—to gain de facto control of the countryside.

I rigged elections, created food shortages & utilized "debtor nation usury tactics." In a greyer capacity, I worked as a "5 o'clock shadow" for a coalition of multi-nats who hid most handsomely their greed & market fervor behind our fair flag. & for one & all I was called upon to supervise multi-stage disseminations of the virus then commonly known as "inebriated consumerism." I peddled any & everything from behind a labyrinth of acrynomous organizations who were able to continually pass along accountability until there was none left to pass around.

My team consisted of a cabal of gimp-minded & mole-eyed pointmen, lobbyists, venture capitalists, organ donor federations, narco-terrorists, weapons specialists, monopoly control feasability experts, State Dept. operatives, interlocking boards of directors, USO entertainers & even a Reichstag banker.

I had pounds of medals, piles of commendations bestowed upon me by men of "the right & the wrong," as we used to say. Mention a multi-nat & I had some inside with them. I met mobsters, commerce moguls, movie producers & the 40 Committee which put into play the fiasco that was Allende's overthrow.

I finally did chuck this, this 11 years of splendid dislocation. I wasn't dumb either, I just caught on slowly. Nothing heroic. Just ran out of patience for putting my life on the line amongst lunatic friendly fire & perilous intelligence contre-currents. Toads were doing while flunks were undoing. Commanding then suddenly remanding. Which all culminated in the Sisters of the Habit mess. & when life no longer resembled a bullet—clean & accurate—&

began, instead, to resemble a shotgun blast, I knew it was time. Time for ejectment.

THREE

Three miles up in the sky of firmament & fluff, amongst the ferrous swirls of the Andes, winds whipping at my limbs, I finally managed to dodge the sophisticated Mobile Tactile Radar (MTR) which uses millimeter wave tech for ultra-detailed surveillance.

So there I stood, on a precipice, hovering & breathing near the Amazon's source. No voice, no wife, no kids, no life. Just an ex-pat renegade with a neuro-magnetic tagging implant tucked in near my pituitary & 200 cm of scar tissue, most of which doesn't even show when I wear a bathing suit. [*& in earnest you agreed to run your finger along some of it that tailed down my neck. With a peacock's tail bundle of furtive café eyes glancing our way. Your finger was cold, betraying nervousness.*] & then there's all the micro-k7 & microfiche data molding in the neuro-surgically modified folds of my cerebrum.

I was really nothing more than an idiot who knew too much gone AWOL. Too much about Drug Enforcement Agency (DEA) manufactured "freedom fighters," Commerce Chambers, the KKK "cloaked in mom's old sheets" & the dark-hooded gangs hired to destabilize rent-controled neighborhoods. I also knew too much about the TPCF (Trilateral Paramilitary Coercive Force), & for that alone they'd love to nose me out & pin me full of serum to the temple, inducing "natural" subdural hematomas. & I'd go out mum & dignified—like Bill Casey.

So, to forget I buried myself in astro-anthropological studies. I tasked away at unravelling the riddle of an outcast band of Incas—purported sunworshipping peacemongers who spoke a rarified tongue, burnished & lovely in their stillness, as if cast in the image of their own visions. Coca-leafed hallucinators who had managed to carve through consciousness to certain yearning mysteries. Arriving at miracles & knowing how to handle them. That's the key—knew how to handle them. [*The commodification of their secrets by huckster-*

evangelicals, it is surmised, led to their eventual demise.] Today we confront so many miracles that our minds refuse to synthesize them. & thus we go awry, fall out of synch with awareness.

& so over some months I was to learn that the mechanics of forgetting was as dangerous & difficult as any technological maladaptation of info. I was forced to eat half my data—stuff that didn't make it back to my Jersey City Post Office Box—when detained in a ceramic detention cell by Bolivian Border Gendarmes. I nearly choked to death in papyrus vomit that came up like plaster.

& since confessions were not forthcoming (I was babbling deliriously, which they gladly mistook for insouciance), the soldiers, barking in baseball English, knocked me around until I'd squatted over a fire fueled by my own notebooks, singeing off most of my haunch hair, & leaving me permanently scarred. It hurt to sit, walk & urinate for months thereafter.

The Gendarmes (dressed in their Nazi–Boy Scout irregulars) eventually tired of their retro-reich toyings & dumped me from an unmarked mini-camion into the glaring street of some outback village. & there I nursed my wounds in the sharp-slanted shadows, in the trickle that had once been the village fountain.

I realized they'd only spared me because they'd discovered my neuro-mag skull implant with its internationally known template—that of the crucifix superimposed dollar sign. They realized that my easy death could mean less military hardware & more trouble than my spared life would.

Amaia, a Geology masters from La Paz, took me in. She was strong & sharp as a jag of porto bottle. A week after we'd met, however, she was cornered, gang-raped, forced to lay with her dead stepfather (bullet through temple). But she did not crack & they dumped her too, from a speeding mini-camion, like a sack of garbage with a dizzy halo of flies buzzing around it. When her story first appeared in various alternative news sources, several organizations, including universities, extended invitations for her to come speak. But when she applied for a U.S. visa they classified her as a security risk.

What I had: evidence that Klaus Barbie, Nazi SS Elite & CIA-warehoused operative, had been ratlined into Bolivia, where he established a potentially embarassing (to the U.S.) clandestine operation, networking neo-Nazi paramilitary mercenaries, funding the venture with a CIA-endorsed cocaine cartel. (Dope-selling gangsters became essential allies in our battle against Communism.) This & many other phosphorescent skeletons in a deep closet, indeed.

FOUR

I also knew that the TPCF had installed their South American base of operation, a massive Teledyne Micronetics Radar Cross Section Range Facility in these hills under the guise of astro-physics research. From here they could "squid" out in any direction. [*This kind of talk had you scribbling so furiously that I couldn't help running my hand through your hair. & this made you back off & realize your professionalism could perhaps be easily compromised.*]

The TPCF was a Trilateral offshoot of YAFers, mercenary hopefuls, seminary rejects, techno-byters & ex-colleagues, all weaned on a diet of info-prowess, Jonestown, sci-fi & 6th grade civics. They operated within the greed-titilating & fear-endowed framework developed by the TPCF Infra-Motivational Skills Unit.

These functionaries were indeed all aliens to this red plateau. Aliens working with the diligence of carpenter ants in their stiff ripstop hydra-perm jump fatigues, which trapped body moisture in hydra-perm cells to cool them in summer, warm them in winter. Or maybe their peculiar mech-gait had something to do with the harnassing of omni-low washover decibel hums as mantras, a tech-extension of chain gang moaning blues.

I'd only been peripherally involved with their activities in places like Siam, Zaire, Berlin & Rio. I'd never actually stepped foot in any of their encampments. So when I first spotted these busy hives struggling with guide wires, girders, huge mesh tumblers filled with silk flowers, my view tended toward the phenomenological. I didn't know what to make of them. It was like seeing my first Dali or Busby Berkley film.

Some carried out structural analyses employing micro-vids. Some drove white crane-lifts wielding huge sections of blindingly incandescent structures (look at a moth flicking around a bright bulb) across the pocked lot. Others busied themselves, with wrenching cables to prevent tarps from flapping wildly in fierce gusts. Mute women transported jiggling glass tubes in oblong black boxes, in what looked like shopping carts cut in half, to a trailer stabilized with a series of electro-hydraulic jacks.

The structures at first made me think of a deflated beach toy. But eventually, in the right crisp light, one got the idea that one was wandering through a brisk fog with crystals hung from its rolling billows. But there was something ELSE about these...floats...these CONstructs. Were they somehow meant to augment the dispensation of spiritual foreign aid? Or were the TPCFers surveillance & neutralization experts? Or just roadies for a traveling construction firm specializing in metaphysical parade floats for all occasions? Promoting world harmony? Creating new CON markets? Teaching New Order CONsumption? Not unlike me? Yes. Yes & yes. But it wasn't always that the con-strat worked as conceived. So, to say they were bad or patriotic or victimizer was never totally right or wrong & depended on a variety

of stimuli & contexts. & thus, I saw them more as victims of their own victimizations.

They can best be described as Midwesterners, college grads with T-bone brains & pinched drawls that personified the tentative sprawl of their topog. Lovelorn & woetorn between their Dodge & their dogma. Lost on the way to god or the fridge. They bandied on about gadgets to get & god to go.

In time I learned to shadow-mingle, lean into their bragadosio. Play in their play because once the crew got it on with a sling of this, a slug of that, every gutter-guzzling whisper, every flickering pulse, pragmatic prayer, flatulent myth, hyper-saturated in post-imperialist nostalgia was "enregistered with impunity" on my micro-corder with its superb macro-compass microphone, in the local dive, La Cañon. Was it all in the name of altruistic muckraking? Well, some of that, & a lot of spite.

Eventually fists would pound the lacquered bar top. Spilled sweet drinks soaked up into hungry laps. [*By this time we were at the bar where I could more forcefully demonstrate my point. & finally you decided to accept my offer of cognac because, as you yourself said, "it's necessary."*] "We're talkin' 62% illiteracy," Stace. "Back aswards, gullible, ready!" Is just a snatch of the garrulous banter, psycho-fallout from those engaged in extremely hi-stress factor-functions. & I know stress. & then I remember that pasty-faced cherub from Fort Wayne, lugworm moustache wiggling in the distressed face of the Kenosha Calvinist "...enlightened rights of purchase...dignified dynamic of the consumer function..." & the Calvinist just shook his head, unsure of what it was exactly that he was agreeing with.

FIVE

But you had to hand it to them. Their fete constructs certainly produced the predicted glittering riffles of hope-hype. They did. They manufactured these floats utilizing the think bank & the input of mass hypnosis strategies as perfected by Holidays On Ice, the CIA Urban Funk Campaign & the Guru Maharaji, 70s mantra misfit.

He'd offered his inside into mass hypno-tech in exchange for immunity from prosecution for tax evasion & religious racketeering charges. They'd been commissioned by Royalty, juntas, parliaments, trade commissions, the Gator Bowl, the World Cup, Idi Amin, Socialists & corporate jubilees.

Their structures (they WERE structures with mass, drag & tangible detail, afterall, weren't they?), their "swirling hoarish oysters with their pearls of eternity" were usually drawn by teams of hi-shouldered pink-eyed Clydesdales covered in armored plates of mirror flexi-glass, a super-lite, breathing polymer. The horses were adorned with Hindu make-up, "a profound, disarming loveliness," bright colored tambourines affixed to their foreankles, as if Shiva or Quetzalcoatl himself were guiding them through the teeming throngs.

Vertiginous trumpeters in bullet-proof seraphic costumes blew brassy, post-jazz elongated epiphanies. The mesmerizing sonority had a noticeable effect on gleestruck bystanders. "March On Christian Soldier" wafted out from undetectable sound sources. This blended subtly with the everyday ambiance of the locale. & everywhere, regardless of regional sophistication quotients, people fell for the CONstruct's spell. Ingenious? Yes. Beguiling? That too. Paris & Vienna went just as enthusiastically as any Manila barrio or Oceania outback.

Bystanders & parade participants claimed "elevations," levitations, heart flutters. Witnesses felt suddenly larger, more chosen, beyond their means. Some were "cured" of senility. Others were freed of their "shackles of dubiosity"—or so the media mindspeak babble-bytes claimed. Personal credit ratings soared! Per capita purchasing power boomed! There were even claims of a Second Coming, of sorts. In town plazas rubberneckers, Christ-und-Allah Pundits, ex-ambulance chasers, kids on dads' shoulders coagulated around where cigar-chomping entrepeneurs, local news-Con-tainment heads vied with dapper neo-heroic land speculators & ladies in lynx for photo opportunities with the CONstructs.

Civic pomp waxed then waned. & the TPCF, in this interim,

would dismantle, pack & make their signature evasive mobile disappearances in grey mini-vans with wraparound *brise-miroir.*

SIX

In Mexico City, site of *Tier Monde* agitations, a cluster of anarcho-studs, urban Redskins, renegade drunk libertaire priests, Villainistas & Mariachi punks pirated the airwaves of a mega-pop radio station & issued ergo-flashes that detailed the machinations of "the sugar-coated Quetzalcoatl hoodwinks" & the hyper-imbalances between desire & availabilty, goods & purchasing power that usually followed the float fetes.

The crackling *quatre-langue* communique found its way to cold Joliet tenements, Trenchtown record shanties, Berlin *polizei* dorms & the "cult bunkers" around Seoul full of acid jazz aficionados in tire-tread sandals. & from these cramped plots, dustbins, cardboard shacks, dung brick huts, rust bowl tenements & war zone banlieues, the squatters, disgruntled grafitoonists, syndical-humanists, Groucho Marxists, girl gangs & Durutti Columnists coagulated into the makings of post-Halloween direct action groups, targetıng the floats to do them irreparable damage.

But these animated, *trop tard* actions played well into the spectacular wisdom web of the governing, who released media tales that filled the consumptive classes with fear. This set off delirious "Long Hot Summer" style looting in Calcutta, Prague, Miami, The Bronx & Brixton. This, in turn, as pre-conceived, set off a vicious process of escalating misconceptions that inevitably opened the gates to redoubled police actions as commanded by bilious politicos, woven as they were into their U.S. aid tie-ins, ordering martial law, random arrests, bans on the sales of intoxicants & instigating "turf integrity" intra-strifing & periodic "stabilizations & arbitrations of non-existence for the collective welfare."

SEVEN

The floats were NOT mana from any heaven or mall. Yes, I know. I know. These elongated flatbed Ford trucks were merely covered in chicken wire to which had been tied thousands of talismanic silk flowers, Michael Jackson mementos, polyethylene moiré *sultra*-thin sheets, subliminal hologrammatical psych-advert tiles, micro-chip-activated tinsel sheaves, tiny diamond-like reflectors designed by commissioned brilliandeers, integrated aural embellishment sound systems, US HPSi PA systems, built-in wail-yelp audio frequency oscillators & other tech "borrowed" from the CIA's "Wandering Souls" aural harassment campaign in Cambodia & expertise purchased from the studios of George Lucas. The 350 mega-watt amp & speakers transmitted behavior-programmed, autosuggestive hope-hype multiple untruths—"Being is Buying, Buying is Being"—broadcast at almost indiscernible vols.

In their conglomeral entirety the floats managed to blur the frontier between interior & ex (is that bad? I don't know), throwing phenomenological precision into disarray, setting the stage for quasi-religious mass suspensions of disbelief.

The most effective CONstruct feature however, was the underbelly-mounted heat-sen release-valve vaporizers, dispensing a thin mycologically fungicidal mist which operates on bio-process time-release degeneration schedules.

At first this aromatic mist was perceived to cause euphoria, giddiness, increased consumption of stupefants & pop enterhype. This was, in part, caused by the restriction of oxygen to the cerebrum. But the long-term contra-indicative effects, although not exactly attributable, are thought to include skin lesions, glandular enlargements, asthma, testosterone realignments, bronchial congestion, & shrinking attention spans.

EIGHT

The TPCF is now history, a disband (or more likely a reconstitution under yet another acronym) that has incurred its own Bay of Pigs. Most of the functionals, after months of debriefing, have been reshuttled into social malls as "normals." Many have stayed on, however, hedging for better pensions, better-entry profiles, or cemetery plots in Arlington. One sells software in Provo. Another tried out for semi-pro football in Akron. One became an airline mechanic in Atlanta. Some acquired total makeover packets—new birth certificates, spouses or spouse equivalents, altered fingerprints, scrambled voice prints.

Some wandered into former folds. Some became repatriated with White Survivalist "Red Dawn" groups. One rumor with some circulation: An appellate judge (ex-TPCF), late for a KKK fundraiser, brazenly arrived at this white robe affair in KKK black magistrate robes.

Funds raised went mainly to para-military camps for Anglo-teens. Here they learn gunhandling, border patrol, ghetto terror & even how to sever heads with sawtooth piano wire. At Camp LeJeune in Alabama, TPCF-spinoff Marines teach splinter White Patriots to use sophisticated weaponry, make explosives disguised as ashtrays, & more.

Various Chambers of Commerce hired TPCF-trained clowns to play the public school circuits to teach hygiene & civics in a fun way. The clowns asked no questions. They were happy to be employed. Laughter was their lifeblood, afterall. The nature of most of the skits & scenarios appeared innocuous, more racial than racist.

NINE

Initially some telepublimeganats showed interest in my writing. Editors-on-limbs, however, desired certain detailed tonedown concessions. No libelous White House references, for instance. Others desired I spice up the love & tragedy angle, tune up the epic potential, the espionage & plunder. With some hacking here, an exploding cigar there, a Mata Hari leftist defector there & a blond hunk of haydom, from I-OW-Aaeee, seduces Mata with his yahoo, cropduster, strafing antics & a houseful of James Bond gadgets (with lucrative ad tie-ins) etc. Well, you see they DID once have notions of making blockbuster stuff of my writing.

Until: Well, yes, I was one of 62 "major political writers" to endorse the spirit of the Villanista-introduced peace (the main idea was to re-invest the governing class with the first person hands-on experiences of the horror of death) resolution as presented to the UN. Since then, my contract with a certain "liberal" NY weekly has been terminated & the tele-film, starring Bruce Dern as myself, has been indefinitely shelved. The roughcut, at this moment, gathers dust on some network warehouse shelf. [*"I don't know," you said from beneath your eyelids heavy as a quilted blanket, "whether to admire you, abhor you, pity you or turn you in."*]

I live comfortably on money earned during my stint with the Committee. My income is supplemented—ironically enough—by my present activities which involve the dismantling of this very Committee apparatus & all its historical maljustifications for continued promulgation (as in Irangate) of the next Chile, Grenada or Wounded Knee.

I still give a goodly number of "rad-lib" lectures on campuses each year. I am always heckled—& praised. That's par for the course. I don't mind. It's sort of amusing, really. Well, at least they're lively & well-attended. I have no qualms about any of this. I toadied, sure, but I don't regret anything—except, possibly the Sisters of the Habit thing. The money lies safe in one bank & it all spends quite easily, thank you. [*I ordered up one more round despite your modest protestations, &, in the course of our contemplative sipping, you said something curious: "You're destined to forever live not in comfort but in the agony of never knowing whether someone else's actions, no matter how genuine, will somehow be used against you. The dread of motivation. Don't you worry about me?"*] No, because, afterall, there are no more saints. Never were. Isn't THAT the truth! Besides, saints, especially the dramatic ones, became saintly only after denouncing their former lives of indulgence & profligacy. & tempted they were. & sinned they did. This made their ascendancy all the more heroic. Isn't it easier to never drink than to give it up once you've become an alcoholic? This is the principle upon which all fine drama stands.

I never worked for the money per se (ignorance or virtue—take your pick), although the cynicism of our times dictates I say just that. Usually to protect senstivities not worth protecting. Although the abhorrent nature of past activities prevents me from returning to my former employers (that & the fact that they wouldn't mind breaking my knees or reprogramming my neuro-mag skull chip), I still have fond memories of adventure, sweat, intrigue & those undeniable paroxysms of power & ecstasy, the true systole & diastole of all life. Ah, to be in the thick of some kinetic to & fro again! [*"But what about love," you asked? "I'm not above believing in miracles," I said. But you didn't get the hint because you did not raise your head up from your notepad & cognac to look into my eyes, as I'd hoped you would.*]

Well, I last made love in 1969. That proverbial Summer of Love. Or maybe it was '68, during the Chi-town riots. Or was it Bangkok in '69? Anyway, all my encounters with chemo-trans-orbital surgery & periodic neuro-flushings of sensitive data have rendered me a mere bystander in this game called love. I am succored only by a few flickering flames. Scratchy images on a battered 8mm film. The last time—yea—in a Bangkok claptrap, wasn't very good anyway. I didn't know at that time that it'd be my last. All I know is that it was a splurge & it was paid for. Which certainly has more to do with who I no longer was, or, rather, who I never allowed myself to be, rather than anything I was, at the time, quickly becoming. OR, for that matter, who SHE was. If I were a painter, the painting I'd do of her would be very nice, mythically so.

Oh, sure, I still dig up dirt, come up with a bone that goes to some skeleton somewhere now & then. I can still ring some bells in some big cathedrals sometimes. Sure, I periodically command a small staff of intern research rats, diligent lefties who scour reams of data for detail & dirt. & I still get hate mail by the kilo. But all this penwiping leaves me dissatisfied. Like perfunctory fellatio. Like a badly prepared meal in a fancy resto. I don't know.

Anyway, I'm left with the distinct impression that I'm not much more than a spayed watchdog on a long moral leash. [*& these were the words I'd hope you would consider while writing your exposé or whatever. & hope will someday haunt the spaces between your words.*] I can carp on about cost overruns, functionary ineptitude, sexism & homophobia in government agencies & they let me bark up that tree because there's no one up that tree because that tree died long ago. & thus my bark goes a long way in proving how truly free we all are. ▼

HITLER'S DOG

Black Sifichi

Thank god those dogs can't talk.
• Hermann Goering

I was very apprehensive about becoming Herr H.'s dog. I'd been given to Herr H. by Martin Bormann, to take his mind off a host of problems.

I am a pedigree Alsatian bitch bred for courage, vigilance & intrepidness. Harmoniously proportioned with uniformly graceful lines & a chest of white fur that contrasts smartly with my dark coat, giving me the dignified elegance of evening wear.

I don't think the term "lucky dog" was invented for me, however. I certainly knew that 3 of his 4 previous canine companions had been pedigrees as well. & they all wound up with one-way tickets to the boneyard via the Augsburg labs, where scientists were busy with such experiments as grafting dog fur to human skin & injecting mutt sperm into women's uteruses. & the 4th? Somehow Socialists had managed to tie explosives to his collar. & he was blown to smithereens near the München Hofbrauhaus, missing Herr H. by mere minutes & meters. Tufts of fur, bright viscera & entrails rained down, draping across ornate railings like wet socks.

Dogs, as you know, are not particularly endowed with free will. But then, neither are soldiers. Oh yes, we're "very intelligent" when we obey commands, leap into a lake, fetch a stick. But is that really intelligence? Pavlov knew better. So did Napoleon.

From time to time you will notice a dog tugging on his leash in a direction quite contrary to that of his master's. That's not free will. That's enslavement to scent.

The portion of a dog's brain devoted to the olfactory system is by far the most sprawling. & since the nose is regarded as the most primitive of the senses, the least muddled by philosophic distraction, it is often the most accurate accountant of phenomena.

Most dogs fall weak to scents, their lives slavishly shackled to their noses. Endlessly tagging territory with their scent, a kind of "scentual grafitti," if you will, making a hobby of cataloguing urine vintages from street corners & fireplugs just as a man might collect butterflies. & you'd never catch me high on street scents or jumping crazily into human crotches to gather & analyze their mysterious acrid odors. Call it breeding. Though I wouldn't have minded a quick snort on occasion, or "muff dive," as mutts of no breeding refer to them.

Our visual horizon includes many regions forgotten & unpainted, a lot of table legs & kneecaps. But much is learned from the kneecap. The way they're shaped informs us about diet during adolescence. Types of perspiration hint at present diet & anxiety levels. A scented kneecap is always nice & reveals a person well attuned to life's more sensual aspects. But it's the nose of an exemplary dog—like the eye of a hawk or scope of a rifle—that becomes a sensory extension, an extrapolation of man's incessant desire to control not only his own destiny but the destiny of others as well.

At the portal of Herr H.'s nostrils one could very well have discovered the fate of an entire continent. During WWI, Herr H. was blinded by mustard gas. It was during his convalescence, sitting in petulant darkness hearing the noise & news of Germany's betrayal that his latent trench visions were transformed into something grander. The attending doctor at the time diagnosed his blindness as hysteria-induced. The return of his vision, via hypnosis, was interpreted by Herr H. as a miracle. A miracle Herr H. felt compelled to act upon.

My nose, after some perfunctory training, became quite capable of sniffing out explosive devices or contraband, be it packed in a sardine tin or lead. This left more than a few officers, including Herr H. himself, awestruck. Here, they thought, was their *überhund*. Here was their symbol for Truth—my nose.

Herr H.'s 54th birthday party lent occasion for me to perform for guests. Everyone drank champagne. Except Herr H., who drank tea & commanded me to do my begging routine. Later I did my "school girl" act & even "sang"—a kind of crooning howl that resembled a song only because Herr H. insisted it did. Herr H. liked me because he could be proud of me.

I became an easy extension of his prowess, proof of his good sense. I wore my studded Swastika collar as proudly as any soldier ever wore his Iron Cross. [A Swastika, by the way, is an ancient Indian symbol signifying the 4 cardinal directions, a symbol of harmony & peace. See "Psycho-Geo-Cato Travels."] I'm sure he chose the Swastika carefully, because Herr H.'s vision of peace far surpassed any dog's or soldier's.

Herr H. rewarded me amply for my "service." Feeding me morsels under the dinner table & stroking my chin for what seemed like days on end. This kind of caressing knew no border nor ism. Pleasure knows no affiliation. I'd do most anything for a stroke. & Herr H. knew that better than anyone.

Most of my subsequent "nose scanning," the infamous ferreting out of "*Joden Vermin*" based on "typical" Jewish odors (using blood, hair, saliva, gefilte fish & urine samples), was reserved mainly for photo opportunities. Here I looked ever the canine symbol of the Reich, an emblem of rectitude, logic & racial superiority. Leni Riefenstahl filmed me for hours. Fussed with my fur. Posed me on hills with magnificent backdrop sunsets—filmed from below I looked even more noble & mythic.

I never, however, engaged in the infamous canine attack tests. Dogs like the one named "Mensch" had been trained to leap, upon the command of "MENSCH! GRAB A DOG!," & gnarl off the sexual apparatuses of naked, cowering men, the breasts of bewildered women & the facial features of the defiant. The amount of time it took victims to bleed to death was duly noted by Reich eugenicists.

I knew that the immutable nature & mystical connotations of blood were always too much for Herr H. He never reveled in the spectacle of execution. He was an intellectual & death was his calculus. Besides he had a very delicate constitution. I know. All my meals were overcooked so there was never the hint of bloody raw meat. For these bloody testimonies might easily have unhinged his rhetoric, all the bravado of the Big Lie, a lie so large & all encompassing that its sheer audacity & magnitude of conception would lead to mass confusion. It maintained a hypnotic quality that would allow the Big Lie to be mistaken for fundamental truth—be it Biblical or biological.

The whole notion of sniffing out the enemy was not only untenable but totally without foundation. It just can't be done. Each individual has his/her own unique blood, sweat—specific olfactory print, if you will. I gave the charade a go because my purpose was to serve, not question. & in no time I won the trust of the innermost circles of the SS. I was a fake with a Pinocchio shnoz, but I had the final word. My snout became Truth in fur & flesh. No passport, nor official letter stood in the way of my nose. Thus, ironically, I managed to condemn many "real" Nazis—&, on the other hand, save the lives of many Jews because fear is fear & I actually could smell fear. Instead of no chance, Jews had a 50-50 chance with me.

Otherwise, I did not suffer from ticks, ringworm, halitosis or mange. I did not howl or whine like muttmate "Wolf." I was obedient, graceful, & athletic. Herr H. often showed me off at the Berghof obstacle course. I darted in & out of mazes, jumped barrels, through hoops. Leaps expected of horses over a 6 foot wooden wall. Routine. & at the end of my Olympian rounds I begged Herr H. for my yummy doggie treats, which I snatched mid-flight time & time again.

Henry Ford, mutual admirer of Herr H. (Herr H.'s office contained portraits of both Frederick The Great & Henry Ford; Herr H. admired not only Ford's assemblyline innovations but the way his private army of goons & capos was so effective against labor agitators & Bolsheviks), was so impressed that he wanted to use me in advertising his automobiles. & Errol Flynn, himself in glorious shape, thought I might be appropriate for his next action film. "Audiences like dogs," he was heard to say over tea on the veranda with Herr H. & Bormann.

Who were all these guests? I did not care. I remembered them mostly by their scents & the treats they bore. & I learned to flatter each with my affections & did not care that this was their way of trying to get through to Herr H. Some of these western reps were just curious to meet the man the German people had made their supernatural Christ. "Hitler is victory itself," Goebbels had once declared. Many more came to do business, wearing nice suits like the ones you see in *Esquire*. Some had big vocabularies, others big wallets. Still others smelled a little too good to trust.

The American visitors were chummy & informal, but they usually smelled very fresh. Like men without history, their aftershaves meant not to heighten or accent who it was they were, but assigned to mask the notion of what it was they were afraid they weren't.

& Americans love dogs. Not the ornamental chachka lap dogs Parisians are so fond of. Or Fraulein Braun's 2 black Scotch Terriers, Stasi & Negus, who were nothing more than "scampering handsweepers" to Herr H. I really came to resent her fickle twins, because anytime they entered into our midst I'd be banished to the lonely corridor. & that's when I began to understand why the other wives so despised Fraulein Braun.

Anyway, I was a real dog. I fetched, lept, hunted & rolled over. & since real men love real dogs they loved me. One well-connected Englishman in particular, used to visit with little wax sacks of lamb kidney. MMMmm. & boot polish, that great English kind, for Herr H., compliments of the Duke & Duchess of Windsor, 2 great admirers of Herr H.

I was privy to top secret meetings, laid out under the table, positioned so that Herr H. could stroke me to calm his nerves & temporarily moderate his tantrums. Thus, I was more than companion. I was therapy.

I loved the rich scent of the polish. Rich enough to trigger sweet reveries under the table & olfactory leaps into former lives.

One chubby American from ITT always wore a fruity cologne which was not particularly becoming to anyone who wasn't a fruit fly. He brought boxes of YumYums, special bonbons for dogs which made me drool. I'd perhaps have killed for them. We dogs are easily made to be fanatical & loyal, & thus we are easy spiritual prosthesis for the esteem-deprived.

This chunky cherub, bearer of numerous gifts, represented a consortium of banks & firms who were interested in financing Herr H. "Business is like a penis: it knows no conscience," I'd heard him chortle. The consortium had been very impressed with the way Herr H. had handled wildcat strikes & economic crises, & dispensed with both Socialists & Communists. In '39 he arrived as the rep for a fraternal order of corporations—Ford, GM, Dupont, Standard Oil, RCA & the Chase & Morgan banks—offering Germany materiel & a tele-communications system nonpareil: phones, intercoms, printers. In exchange, these companies (their tankers & overseas HQs) were to receive safe haven from the ravages of war, their investments protected for the mutual benefit of all.

All this rather bored me. But I knew humans got all worked up over this kind of thing, & I let them. I preferred more sublime pre-occupations. Example: although dressed to the hilt, this ITT man farted like crazy. To me a fart is a fart. But also something else—a rich bouquet, an olfactory print revealing dining habits, in his case, a pre-occupation with aphrodisiacs—oysters, ginger, cognac, chocolate-covered strawberries—as well as hints of A-level anxiety. All from his farts!

He'd once made light of his gregarious flatulence by joking, "When people fart they are all equal." To which Herr H., a troubled flatulator himself, responded, "But some are more equal than others." & in amongst the uproarious laughter a deal was struck. The "fat flatulator" was, it turns out, a letch with a weakness for women & drink. Herr H. gained industrial assistance & numerous perquisites for the Reich by offering concubines chosen from the Joy Division, a unique branch of the concentration camps used to accommodate the amorous demands of the Reich & their guests. "Jew-cy Conc-Jew-bines!" The ITT man was heard to spew.

During the day I often played with Gudrun, Himmler's daughter. She knew nothing of history & business. She liked to dance, often taking up my forepaws to do our special jitterbug. I loved her flapping pigtails, pleated skirts, girly smells, & clean white socks, on which I'd tug to tease her. I was versatile. Tough but tender.

I remember the stiff cut of Herr H.'s uniform too, the kind of sartorial precision that beckons images of control & probity. This illusion of prowess was already so ironically betrayed by the ever encroaching realities that it rendered Herr H. pitiable to all but the most faithful. His right arm was, by now, almost totally devoid of function.

Yet on the day Greta Garbo came to visit, his uniform, or him in it, with a colorful rearrangement of medals & an upturned collar, looked quite dashing. Like a polished luger in a velour pouch. A smart Napoleonic curl sat on his forehead like a serpent's tail. He looked rakish, mischievous even—like a boy. Although devoted to Herr H., his generous affections & geography of intriguing odors, I had much difficulty imagining him as a child full of snot & glee. Anyway, there was indeed more to life than just order & discipline.

When Mlle. Garbo, glam-eyed, sultry Salomé, arrived (she'd already been there in Herr H.'s schemes & blood throbbing reveries for days) she was not required to submit to the usual intense search of person. Her person was some ultra-entity beyond mere mortal suspicion. Nor did I get to sniff-search her. You just don't with a goddess. Simple as that.

He was so polite, charming & bashful. Not himself. He even managed to make his right arm come alive long enough to take her hand & kiss it.

He offered her tea (as neither drank), apple cake, chocolate. He showed her huge sprawling maps with bold sweeping arrows. How he'd skirted the fabled Maginot Line. How Czechoslovakia was his little puzzle piece. She sipped her tea. Hid behind the cup, decidedly disinterested in his maps. His advances. She asked nothing of Herr H. & his tousled hair thrusts into deep misunderstood blood-lands. & she spoke only when spoken to. She did not smile & her eyes remained intense as a blue flame.

When I licked her hand she responded quite appropriately by

stroking my ears, petting my hindquarters—which is certainly among my top 5 G-spots. I did not dislike her. But she stroked me hesitantly, perfunctorily as if preoccupied. It just never got beyond mutual respect. She smelled great though. Great is not the word. Not loud or ostentacious. Simply a scent primed to accent the confidence, further cultivate the mystique that oozed from her pores. Images of North Africa, balsam, myrrh, an autumn forest bed, a bed of pine needles & silk & fur, the velvet curtain at the opera. Like her scent, she was impossible to pin down.

It was only some time after the war, that it was reported that Mlle. Garbo had, in fact, had reason for her hesitancy. She'd been packing. Packing a cheap pearl-handled single shot pistol (only good at short range but perfect for concealing in stocking tops). That she had intended to shoot Herr H., my provider, shocked not only me. Gertrude Traubl, Herr H.'s youngest & prettiest secretary, was absolutely devastated by the deception. She could not conceive why anyone would want to harm Herr H. Neither could I. The apparent scheme: Mlle Garbo was to offer Herr H. "a very intimate gift." She'd reach under her dress as if to offer him her garter or more. Instead, in the stocking top sat the tiny pistol. But somehow the occasion never arose. (I like to think it was my presence.)

But even I, to tell you the truth, with my vaunted nose, just had no idea! But what do you want? I was off duty. & I may have a great nose but that doesn't mean I have x-ray vision. I can't read minds, you know.

October 1, 1944: Herr H. denies validity of Dr. Giesing's diagnosis detailing eardrum puncture & possible inner ear damage. Dr. Giesing suggests pain is informing or DEforming some of Herr H.'s critical acumen. Giesing discovers Herr H. empty-eyed on his spartan bed. Herr H. complains of headaches & intestinal pain. Giesing's prognosis: hi-strychnine-toxicity from excessive intake of little black anti-gas pills. His eyes & skin are yellow. Complete physical reveals jaundice—& fact that his sexual apparatus is intact & quite normal, despite vicious already well circulated "1-ball" rumors. Herr H.

requests "more of that cocaine stuff." Giesing, during course of extensive conversations with Herr H., discovers horrific "intellectual inadequacy & petty subjectiveness" that informs Herr H.'s Master Plan. Disgusted, Giesing decides to kill Herr H. with double dose of cocaine rubbed into interior of his nostrils. (Imagine, 10 million souls' suffering hinged on this 1 gesture.) But plan is aborted when valet, Heinz Linge, barges into bedroom unexpectedly.

January 17, 1945: By now Herr H. & Family (clique of sycophants) are living in decidedly less splendid quarters in & under the Reich's Chancellery, lying under 6 feet of earth & 11 reassuring feet of concrete. Windows covered with cardboard. Corridors flooded & offices devoid of paintings, tapestries & carpet. Herr H. is progressively more absent-minded which was to my advantage, because he now fed me 4 or more times a day!

March 1: 3 flights under Chancellery lies bunker for The Family. One traverses duck boards across 1 foot of water to first floor. Another long soggy-carpeted stairway curves down to the 2nd floor of 12 rooms & general mess hall, to the Führer-bunker, 50 feet below, which consisted of 18 cubicles (with its low 6-foot ceilings which made 1 & all appear bigger or other than who they were) separated by a hall, conference & waiting rooms. To the left of the conference room was the map room & the 6-room suite of Herr H. & Fraulein Braun.

March 8: Herr H. in surrounding hills, in a Volkswagen, rubs cocaine along his gums & the lining of his nostrils. Then daydreams of his secret weapon—the atom bomb.

March 16: Sunshine crashes through remaining Chancellery windows. Herr H. paces while phonograph plays "Götterdamerung." He spends hours staring at the portrait of Frederick The Great. His left hand now trembles noticeably. Right arm stiff as a stick. Braun spends day fidgeting with her hair & changing clothes in front of mirror. She wraps naked body with coveted silver fox fur coat. Equates the glamour of the Reich with Hollywood. Herr H.'s trembling hand strokes me with decided lack of involvement. Face pale.

Voice weak & hoarse. We seldom play any more.

April 6: Braun gives herself manicure & pedicure. Wears open-toed shoes to dinner to show off toes. No one but me notices. But I'm not about to fawn over the toes of an adversary. Herr H. throws tantrums. Everyone's confused. Embarrassed. For all of Germany? Or something slightly more circumscribed?

April 20: Last photo of Herr H. reveals a man absorbed by a sooty shadow, as if his body was already being drained into the chiaroscuro ether. He's nearly featureless, non-existent.

April 22: Berlin almost totally surrounded now. Herr H. declares, "the war is lost," in trembling voice. He collapses. Eyes go blank. Braun takes his hand in hers. Smiles like a mother might at her frightened son & says, "I shall stay with you." His eyes suddenly begin to sparkle. He reaches up & kisses her on the lips. At this instant the guests are shocked by realization that their Christ-like Herr H., celibate conservator of Ur-semen, & Braun have been living out of wedlock!

April 23: Fraulein Braun no longer hums. Her cheerfulness evaporates. Air of subdued quiet. Declares: "It's enough to lose one's faith in God." No one sure exactly what "it" is. She composes letter to her sister. Instructs her to bury all Herr H.'s letters in watertight pack in backyard. She strokes me for first time in over 6 months. I'm confused. Corpses of former beings with smiles & aspirations litter streets. Many are repeatedly run over by various retreating or advancing vehicles.

April 24: Himmler attempts to sway Allies to fight Russians together. Many in Berlin claim to see Herr H., saber drawn, fighting a gnarling battle to the last. Herr H.'s personal adjutant burns last of his private letters. Braun refuses to get up for lunch. Spends day examining blemishes in mirror & rummaging through her wardrobe. Young Werewolves, Nazi youth partisans, prowl the Berlin streets for traitors to shoot or hang from lampposts with bold signs hung around wrenched necks declaring their "crimes."

April 25: Berghof partly demolished by Allied bombs. Blasted tin roof flutters noisily in breeze as eerie twisted testimony to the damage. Herr H. relates dream of having army hold out until May 5 to effectively "enlarge the misery of the desperately loyal" so that he can die on same day Napoleon died.

April 26: Herr H.'s arms twitch ceaselessly. He raves & weeps as the huge scope of his destiny as Father of Bloodland constricts, whittles down to the mere owner of a hemmorhoidal malfunctioning fundament. Eyes glassy like the windows of an abandoned building. Totally immersed in drama of personal betrayal by his staff. Braun alters a formal dress to make it more modern. Herr H. pins Iron Cross on a young boy in shorts for blowing up advancing Russian tank. Young boy turns to leave & collapses from exhaustion. I lick the boy's legs.

April 27: News reaches bunker of Mussolini & his mistress being gunned down by partisans near Dongo. Herr H. declares he will not be taken alive: "to be put in some Russian cage." I urinate on corridor carpet. Nerves. He bends over me—his bloated face covered with red splotches—to chide me: "Look me in the eye Blondi, have you betrayed me like my generals?" Don't know what to do. I lick his lifeless hand but to no avail. Herr H. wonders if our ceiling will hold. If the sky will hold. In reprisal for Himmler's betrayal Herr H. has Himmler's liaison officer, Fegelein, shot at bunker entrance. Herr H. misses the execution but feels better knowing it has been carried out. I've lost him. A dog without a bone, a dog without a stick to fetch. Oh, how I yearned for a leash that would tug me this way or that. Women on the street fight over hunks of rancid butter.

April 28: Frau Goebbels declares, "A world without Herr H. & National Socialism would not be worth living in." Women & girls are ordered to the front lines. Herr H. wants to hear none of this. Goebbels yells "Pure Hysteria!" over & over around the bunker. The ventilators suck in brown dusty hot air, dense with the acrid spice of spent explosives. Herr H. broods in sanctity of map room, moving around armies that no longer exist. Braun emerges from her bedroom wearing black silk taffeta gown. I'm surprised. Herr H.

arrives, looking painfully like a splintering toy soldier in uniform. Berlin is bright, not with jubilation but with buildings on fire. In those fires Boticelli's *Madonna & Angels,* Van Dyck's *Diana Surprised By Saturn,* Goya's *The Monk* & hundreds more burn to char.

April 29: Frau H. (née Eva Braun) in smart grey suit that murmurs around her curvaciousness (some wonder about the propriety of her diamond-studded watch) gives her prized fox fur to Traudl. Says; "I always like to have well-dressed people around me." Midnight; Herr H. tells jokes, everyone laughs. He drinks Tokay, a souvenir from a more glorious time. The phonograph plays "Red Roses." The Family is giddy, drunk on gallows humor. There's furious smoking & Schnapps & spirits spilled down chins & dress fronts. Prussian generals cast off their tunics & dance wildly with stenographers. One major tears down huge velvet curtain & becomes a campy countess. Herr H. ceremoniously hands out phials of cyanide to all except loyal valet Linge (11 years of impeccable service). This brings a gurgling giggle to Braun's lips. He apologizes for not having nicer "going away presents." Everyone chuckles. Frau H. declares, "It's so simple. You just bite into this," displaying the capsule in pinch of her well-groomed fingers. "& poof! It's all over."

Goebbels wonders if phials are still effective. Doctor Stumpfegger suggests one be tried on me! & Herr H. agrees! Doctor forces phial into my mouth with a pair of tongs, then cracks phial. Although I collapse I do not die. In the course of my admirably faked death I overhear some less than complimentary things about me expressed by Frau H. & others. I'm left behind to be buried by staff members.

April 30; 1 A.M.: Herr H. bids farewell with glazed, faraway eyes. Shakes hands of faithful. I am hidden in a closet in the H.'s suite, already totally forgotten in the tense hubbub. Folly informing outrage, outrage informing insanity. This saddens me, but also saves my life. News filters in: Mussolini's & mistress's bodies strung up by feet in the lot of a Milan gas station. Citizens invited to kick them in the head. There's boisterous dancing in adjacent rooms. Bormann pleads for calm. Goebbels mumbles on & on about "Pure Hysteria!" Fat greasy smoke envelopes Berlin. Extra tobacco rations issued to placate citizens.

Russians infiltrate the Berlin Zoo. Herr H. eats enjoyable lunch of grey vegetable gruel with his 2 secretaries & cook. He tries to disguise the lameness in his arms, his stooped back & the morphological fact that he had become the crumbling embodiment of his own Reich—the despair of death in the guise of composure. Herr H. gives orders for disposal of corpses. "Where's the woollen blankets?" Herr H. shouts.

Frau H. emerges in her favorite black dress with freshly groomed hair. He says; "You'll be a beautiful corpse but glorious devastation is what I want to illuminate my finish." He demands 200 liters of gasoline. His adjutants inform him that 200 liters just can't be found. Herr H. fumes, "Then siphon it from wrecked vehicles if necessary. Because I do not want to end up exhibited in a Russian Wax Museum!" Valet Linge holds final door open to the cramped 6x9 quarters. After Braun passes he says to Linge, "You must live for the sake of my successor." Linge is stunned.

3:30 P.M.: Herr H. bids farewell to bodyguards & joins Frau H. on the couch of their suite. She gazes at Herr H. He grips her knee as she cracks the plastic phial of potassium cyanide between her teeth. In minutes she is dead. The brass hull of the phial falls to carpeted floor. She slumps away from Herr H. (so his death can be the glorious centerpiece) over the arm of a chair, lips closed tight, nostrils discolored by cyanide.

3:36 P.M.: Herr H. strokes dead wife's hair, picks up his old 7.65 caliber Walther he has carried since Beerhall Putsch days to protect himself from Bolsheviks & garner attention in crowds. He fondles finely-crafted handle, staring at the framed photo of his mother as a young woman. Puts barrel to his right temple & pulls trigger. His body pitches forward, in right corner down across the coffee table. The Walther lies almost neatly on the table. A 6.35 mm back-up pistol lies under the table. Left arm knocks over pitcher of water, some of which soaks into Frau H.'s black dress.

I emerge from the closet, full of trepidation. Sit by my master's side all alone. This man who had fed me so well, even in last difficult days. & when he'd called upon me to do just one last thing for him & the Reich I had failed. Another more basic instinct had compromised my loyalty to both master & Fatherland.

I lick his hand & discover gaping exit wound in right temple oozing dura & brain matter. A small puddle of thick dark blood gathers on the carpet. & here was I, dumb dog, trying to lick Herr H. awake, unable to comprehend the philosophic or historical magnitude of his death—or ANY death, for that matter.

It's much simpler for me. I had grown so familiar with his smell & even in death he smelled like the Herr H. of old. & I liked blood. I am, afterall, first cousin to the wild *canis lupus*, an animal susceptible to ancient instincts.

When Bormann & Linge burst into the suite they're suitably spooked. Unsure of what their eyes are seeing. Me, Blondi, dead Blondi, still alive, licking the bullethole clean. At first I don't budge. But Goebbels' voice is filled with the kind of anger that usually emerges from the maw of panic.

Linge & Kempka carry Herr H. out, wrapped in a grey Army blanket. & I watch from the Bunker entranceway as Russian artillery send dust & rubble from the crumbling Chancellery walls raining over us. Red hot embers arc across my view like shooting stars.

They lay him down in the trench a mere 10 meters from the bunker entrance. Adjutant Kempke adjusts Herr H.'s trousers. Then lays Frau H. to his left. Kempke touchingly fixes her hair as if preparing her for a photo shoot. He moves Herr H.'s arm to his side to make him more comfortable & dignified. Debris continues to rain over us. They pour can after can of gasoline over the bodies. Kempke lights a rag & tosses it onto the bodies. Ball of flame so intense it warms my snout. They stand mesmerized, unable to speak. Frau H.'s dentures melt out of her grimace.

That night they scrape charred remains into a canvas sack with cardboard that had once covered a Chancellery window. Drop it into a shellhole already occupied by dumb muttmate, "Wolf." They cover the hole with sand, stone & rubble, jumping on it to pound it down. It looks like an odd ritualistic dance around a configuration of jagged, crumbling dolmen. & shortly thereafter Berlin surrenders.

May 1, 1 A.M.: Frau Goebbels drugs her 6 children with spirits then places crushed ampules of potassium cyanide in their mouths, as if performing communion.

I sit on the burial site of Herr H. At dawn I watch an SS officer shoot the Goebbels in the garden. Officer stares at his own hand attached to the gun & the gun to death & death to fate. Then hurriedly they douse the Goebbels with gasoline & light the pyre. & then torch the bunker. I watch remaining uncaptured ragtag members of the Family flee. Gertrude Traudl in silver fox & several officers in formal evening wear. Kempke implores me to follow.

But I remain behind on the tamped earth where underneath lies my Herr H. until Russian troops arrive. I watch one young soldier take aim at me. I see the squint eye through the aimsight just as he sees me—face to snout. They, of course, want to shoot me. I don't blame them. Me with mouth caked in dried blood, looking dazed & rabid, as if guarding some secret Nazi bower.

But suddenly something comes over me. I don't know what. My ears go soft. Proud shoulders go into a slouch. My tail wags in true Academy-Award-style. In fact, it's as if my tail's wiggling my entire hindquarters, as if my very life depends on it, & it probably does. Some of the soldiers ultimately relent, go soft, squat down, rifles in the dust, & lure me over.

A young soldier, not yet 18, the one with the aimsight in his eye, applies a certain touch. Has an instinct for stroking, knows right away how it's done, even offers me a tin of pork paté. I lick his hands & the hands of his friends as a sign of submission & my need for salt, & in no time I'm their mascot. An indispensible tool of the Allies.

I had, afterall, a very keen nose for Nazis. Which really meant I knew where many of them had gone into hiding. Which, once again, lent credence to the power of my mythic nose. Although, once again, I was cheating.

In the following days I helped root out several dozen key Nazis. (2 dead Herr H.'s were being found on average daily.) Yes, among them some number of Herr H.'s personal staff. I recognized them as they were marched—*hande hoche!*—along the rubble-covered streets. & they undoubtedly recognized me too. Burning houses lit up rubble-filled streets. & it can be surmised that some became enlightened just then, just as they recognized me, me being petted by my new friends. We see a woman with 2 shopping bags full of bricks tied to her wrists & grasping a baby under each arm, leap into the Havel River.

& I hear the abrupt burp of machine gun fire. My ears still sensitive to the clean pop-pop-pop. Then they're dead. Dead with their several minutes of enlightenment—that short span of time between when they'd spotted me & realized I was the snitch, until the lead actually entered their chests.

& I could smell the wall, the wall against which their shoulder blades had rested, that funny sulphurous smell of when bullets hit brick & cement. ▼

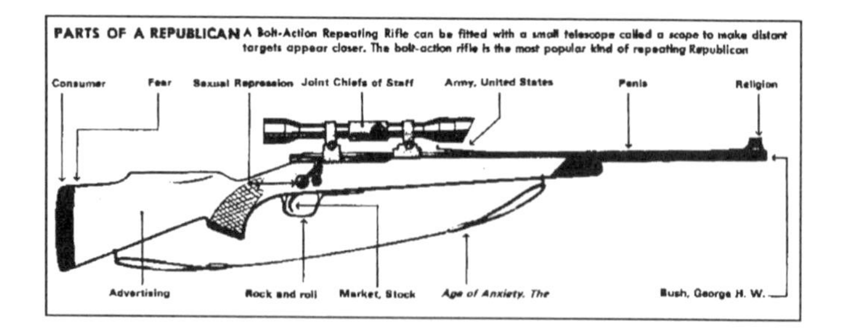

BEAT THE DUTCH NOW!

For Cool Sleeping in Humid Java, Nothing Beats a "Dutch Wife"

The girls, resting in their bedroom, straddle kapok-filled *rolkussen*, or round cushions (Dutch wives), which absorb perspiration. Netherlanders follow this custom throughout their tropical empire. Even those living in the United States find the bolsters a comfort in summertime.

found

> ***The Dutch seem very happy & comfortable but it is the happiness of animals.***
> **• Samuel T. Coleridge**

I am the appointed spokesperson for D.A.B.L., the Dutch Anti-Bashing League, & I am more than a little perturbed & peeved that we Dutch people must daily withstand the omnipresent barrage of invective in an Anglo world littered with bile-laden pejoratives ("The devil shits Dutchmen." Samuel Pepys once said.) & scurrilous aspersions that demean & impugn the noble character of the NEDERLANDER.

Thus it is before you that I wish to present my case. Be aware, however, that the virulent & caustic nature of some of the following profanities may offend some among you. Please consider this your warning.

Many of the subsequent phrases were pejoratively introduced during the 17th & 18th centuries by the British. They are based in their trade rivalry, cultural differences, naval jealousy & prejudice toward their Channel rivals, we—the NEDERLANDER, the Dutch. They are well documented & have all, to some degree, infected our daily lexicon. For instance, a:

Dutch Cure = Suicide.
Dutch Talk = Gibberish.
Dutch Treat = Each pays his own.
Dutch Feast = Party where the host gets drunk before the guests.
Dutch Bargain = One-sided.
Dutch Courage = False courage, bravado inspired by drink.
Dutch Cheer = Liquor.
Dutch-buttocked = Cattle with very large hind quarters.
Dutch Fuck = Lighting one's cigarette from another's lit cigarette.
Dutch Kiss = Indulgence in sexual intimacies.
Dutch Build = Thick set body type.
Dutch Cheese = Bald-headed person.
Dutch Reckoning = A bad day's work.
Dutch Widow = A whore.
Dutch Wife = A round cushion which absorbs moisture placed between thighs when napping.

Dutch Wife = Board with a hole in it used for male onanistic satisfaction.

Dutch by injection = Said of a woman living with a foreigner.

Double Dutch = Speech very difficult to understand.

Dutch Oven = Farting in bed & then lifting the blankets.

Beat The Dutch = To be incomprehensible or surprising, do something remarkable.

Do a Dutch = To run away, abscond.

In Dutch = In trouble or disfavor.

The Dutch have taken Holland = To impute stale news.

I Am A Dutchman = I am not who I am.

Old Dutch Clock = Wife.

That Beats The Dutch = That beats everything.

Dutch Uncle = 1 who criticizes or reproves with severe frankness.

Dutchman = An irregular lump in brown sugar.

Dutchman = A piece or wedge inserted to hide the fault in badly made joint to stop an opening .

Dutchman's Anchor = Anything that's needed & has been left behind.

Dutchman's Fart = Sea urchin.

Dutchman's Headache = Drunkenness.

Dutchman's Land = An illusory land mass on horizon caused by presence of cloud bank or like haziness.

The Dutch Boare Dissected, or a Description of

HOGG-LAND.

A *Dutch man* is a Lusty, Fat, two Legged Cheese-Worm: A Creature, that is so addicted to Eating Butter, Drinking fat Drink, and Sliding, that all the World knows him for a lusty Fellow. An *Hollander* is not an *High-lander*, but a *Low-lander*; for he loves to be down in the Dirt, and *Boar*-like, to wallow therein.

However common the preceding may be, they are no less offensive. The following phrases are more troublesome as to their derivation, allusion or intent:

Dutchman's Shower = To urinate on oneself (esp. when inebriated.)
Dutchman's Shoeshine = To urinate on one's shoes.
Dutch Erection = When one sits down & one's pants front "tents" or puffs out.
Dutch Vagina = Coin purse.
Dutch Prosthesis = A handle on a beer mug.
Dutch Abortion = To vomit after imbibing.
Dutch Orgasm = Electroshock therapy.
Dutch Semen = Beer head.
Dutch Ejaculation = Scraping excess head off a beer
Dutch Marriage = Drunken, unconsummated 1-night stand.
Dutch Handshake = Masturbation.
Dutch Braille = Indiscriminate bosom fondling or breast grabbing.
Dutch Nipple = Pimple.
Dutch Date = Leaving obscene phone messages on another's answering machine.
Dutch Fun = Automobile accident caused by drunk driving.
Dutchman's Shovel = Penis.
Dutch Laugh = Gas, indigestion, intestinal cramps.
Dutch Spice = House dust, soot.
Dutchman's Toupée = Ill-fitting hat.
Dutchman's Necktie = Hangman's noose.
Dutch Intellectual = A barking dog, on a short leash, in a small backyard.
Dutch Priest = Bartender.
Dutch Pope = A drunk banker at a party.
Dutch Pornography = Baby pictures.
Dutch Husband = Dildo.
Dutch Fellatio = Vacuum cleaner.
Dutch Jazz = A scratched phonographic record.
Dutch Poetry = Balancing one's accounting books.
Dutch Political Slogan = "Beer Here!" (Later appropriated by

Yankee Stadium Concession Vendors.)
Dutch Astrology = Yesterday's news or newspaper.
Dutchman's Diet = Watery soup served with a fork.
Dutch Love = Remove socks, close eyes, open mouth, place hands in pockets, steal one another's pocket change.
Dutch Duet = One man farting, another burping.
Dutch Take-out = Take out the garbage.
Dutch Gift = Socially transmitted disease.
Dutch Summer = August 1-August 2.
Dutch Paramour = Farm animal.
Dutch Pet = Fleas, crabs or other pests.
Dutch Mansion = Toilet.
Dutch Carnival = Town dump.
Dutch Patriarch = Midwife.
Dutch Red Wine = Menstruation. (as in: "Honey, you spilled the Dutch Red Wine again.")
Dutch White Wine = Sour milk.

The following sayings are doubly disturbing because they seem ever vague while still insinuating aspersive intent:

I invited 6 Dutchmen & 7 pairs of shoes showed up.
He makes love like a Dutchman in a butcher shop.
After I told her I loved her she looked at me with cheeks of Dutch jelly.
Making love with her was like smoking a Dutch cigarette.
I was high as the Dutch hills of Eindhoven.
He walks like he's carrying a valise full of Dutch beef.
A Dutchman is like one fart with a shoe.
Like a drunk Dutchman in a laundromat.
It's like dodging a Dutchman's spit.

The list goes on I'm afraid. I relay this truncated list to you in hopes that we can mutually agree on the notion that any nationality or race maligned & denigrated in such a fashion can only mean that all peoples of all nations are maligned. I thank you all for your kind attention. ▼

I HAD SEX WITH ANDY WARHOL UNTIL HIS WIG FELL OFF

Dix/10

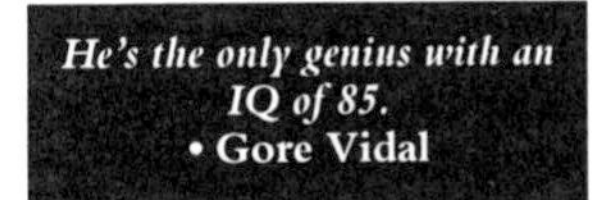

The wig is rare & missing. It had been one of 99 wigs in the Warhol Estate Collection: 11 each of 9 styles. Mr. Warhol had discovered this aforementioned & now missing gem in an Upstate NY garage sale. It was described as a capless "Freedom Power" wig, which is oft regarded by periwig specialists as "tough enough to turn on ANY man, be he miner, monk or martyr." & has often been regarded as THE essential spark that ignited the initial 60s "Black Pride" movement. It is made of 100% miracle modacrylic.

The wig (catalogue #1122-A) has been the subject of much art market speculation of late. Art commodities experts estimate the missing wig would easily top $45,000 on the auction block. Much of the inflationary interest is no doubt due to the fact of its untimely & mysterious disappearance.

This same wig, coincidentally, has also been the choice of the Latin American arm of the CIA since 1974. They regularly recommend this particular style over all others for their counter-insurgency Third World allies. Reference is, in fact, made to it in the *Psychological Operations In Guerilla Warfare* Manual, which is largely devoted to semi-violent decoy & transvestite coercion tactics, tactics consistent with stated U.S. foreign policy. This wig supplies numerous footnotes to the purported Hispanic penchant for women with voluminous "afros" & ample glutei maximi.

It seems amply clear that on our fateful, & largely anti-climactic, eve Mr. Warhol had been particularly titillated by the high cross-cultural kitsch factor of the particular fete we attended together, which honored 4-star general, Panama campaign media pet, art collector & arms dealer, General John Vasectome.

Mr. Warhol had been particularly taken by the ostentatious combination of brass Pakistani table ornaments, lacquered Mexican Mariachi musicians in sombreros, Japanese fortune scrolls, red Swiss Valentine doilies, 400 mermaid candles donated by a Taiwanese electronics magnate & 250 coral-studded pewter goblets flown in by hostess Joan Herring on 3 private jets from the Canary Islands.

Pre-arousal Warhol had reveled in the details of the feast disaster when, 1 course into the elaborate 6-course meal, 3 trays of carmelized sorghum sugar baskets filled with pomegranate sorbet collided with a tray of swordfish eyes floating in a chartreuse flambé jelly, which, in its own turn, ignited several of the guests' Japanese fortune scrolls.

Kitsch recall was a more effective self-arousal tactic than any other method at my fingertips. It reminded me of Lou Reed's comments in '85, when he alluded to Mr. Warhol's eccentric foreplay techniques in terms of the rise of 20th century fascism. He referred to the phenomenon as "auto-oblivia," a spiritual exhaustion steeped in the notion that neither American nor British citizens were aware that their fantastic achievements in prosperity were almost totally dependent on the degradation & exploitation of millions of unskilled laborers, both at home & abroad, workers held prostrate in "abject poverty by the insatiable Western desires for comfort & material acquisition." Or so I remember Reed putting it.

Lou Reed's words ring chillingly true even to this day, as my mind (be it in the unemployment line or the check-out line) endlessly mulls over my past conjugal torments with Mr. Warhol. I remember his recumbent body, campily & cinematically flung across his art deco love seat. & his sickly diminutively dimensioned & arrogantly flaccid member as he reverted to his by now renowned & oft imitated posture of empty palette. His nihilistic corpus stylishly replete of all function, like a man intent on starving his brain of oxygen by refusing to breathe, all in an attempt to cover up the facts of his psycho-sexual dysfunction. I only ever accomplished minimal arousal response from him (despite my ambi-sexual bilateral reputation) utilizing rubber-gloved mechanical ejaculatory pump-action techniques.

& through it all the pseudo-aroused & utterly microphobic Warhol corpus always seemed more likely to break into a yawn than into convulsion. He had, afterall, often referred to love as "mouth to mouth germ warfare."

The endless replay of 60s TV commercials did little to stimulate electro-capillary engorgement. & thus our relationship came to that rude but, I must say, welcome denouement, when his famous "Freedom Power" wig tumbled to his freshly refinished parquet floor that late eve of the General Vasectome Roast. Mr. Warhol even tried to retrieve the spectacle of the moment when he re-enacted one of the cinematic & semiotically-charged swoons of Jean Harlow.

None of you probably ever suspected that Mr. Warhol enjoyed romping gingerly around his apartment like a semi-clad sylvan nymph in his #1201-B wire-base Wonder Wiglet made by the renowned RC Hair Fashions of Omaha. Well, he did. He really did. I just wish I'd had the foresight to save the photos.

This particular model has a very special push-up base to allow for a wide array of winsome styles. It is super thick & long, to provide for a maxi-cascade of shimmering tresses made of 100% human hair from Manila. All of which seemed to echo Mr. Warhol's fervent belief in spiritual materialism. Mr. Warhol, in fact, absolutely adored shaking that bonus 6.5 ounces of hair, which replicated for him a particular voluptuousness that seemed to be so absolutely stifled in his public, evasionary non-life.

The public Warhol (as you may well know) always preferred the ultra-famous lite ash-blonde wig (catalogue #1336-A). "Fave 'do #6," he'd command from the utter worthlessness of his spectacular repose. He, in fact, never appeared in public without it. This particular model, of which there were 11, seemed to heighten that strategic veneer of impenetrable & trademark blandness.

Each of these 11 #1336-A style wigs is made of 100% human hair. The ideal human hair for which he personally searched long & hard. Mr. Warhol, at 1 point, in September of 1968, I recall, began to correspond with one Larry David Jennings. Mr. Jennings had sent Mr. Warhol a photo of himself, as stipulated by an ad Mr. Warhol had placed in the Personal Ads section of *Screw*. Although Mr. Warhol was never known to be particularly romantic, he was capable of stimulating a certain quasi-romanticism through the utilitarian exchange of product for favor. Mr. Warhol implored Mr. Jennings to grow his hair to a specified length. Then have it cut & sent to Mr. Warhol via Express Mail. Mr. Warhol, in exchange, vowed to arrange a power law firm to handle his appeals process.

Mr. Jennings began supplying the hair for the trademark ash blond mop wigs from his Huntsville, Texas Death Row cell, while Mr. Warhol's lawyers succeeded in prolonging Mr. Jennings' appeals process. Mr. Jennings had been found guilty in 1964 of torching his wife's poodle, then bludgeoning her to death with a refrigerator door & then killing her parents with a Phillips head screwdriver. [Forensics experts counted over 200 puncture wounds.] Yet, he fervently maintained his innocence right into 1976, when suddenly his appeals process seemed to dry up.

Mr. Jennings had always been very grateful to Mr. Warhol; Mostly for help & support that Mr. Jennings only imagined. In prison he managed to familiarize himself with the art of Mr. Warhol & decided he too liked the way cereal boxes & beer cans looked, & so thought that were they to meet they'd have plenty to talk about. But he never met Mr. Warhol personally until April 12, 1976, when arrangements allowed for Mr. Warhol to be presented in person with Mr. Jennings' 10th Ziploc Baggie of ash-blond clippings. This was to be his last contribution to the Warhol Periwig collection, because Mr. Jennings' had already placed his order for his Final Meal—an entire pepperoni pizza, Greek salad, large slice of 7-layer chocolate cake & a Dr. Pepper. (The same remorseless meal, it has been strongly suggested, he calmly consumed over the dead body of his wife.) Later on that very same day, Mr. Warhol joined the privileged members of the press & bitter survivors of his wife's family to witness the pulling of the proverbial switch.

Some say Mr. Warhol cynically let up on the appeals process when it became clear that Mr. Jennings would supply him with his much anticipated 10th crop of hair. Some of these same people claim that Mr. Warhol had, in fact, petitioned the Appeals Review Board months in advance for a good seat at the execution. Thus far, records do not bare out these slanderous accusations.

Others claim that his Electric Chair litho series was inspired not by politics but by his special relationship with Mr. Jennings. (Afterall, wasn't it Mr. Warhol who had created that *haute* scene equation: stylish boredom = fashionable politics?) In fact Mr. Warhol once told me that he was grateful to Mr. Jennings because he had sucked all the painful emotion that could ever be associated with executions out of that particular spectacle. This, Mr. Warhol reasoned, made it easier to go on living.

Mr. Warhol later confided that the mere thought of wearing this ash-blond mop wig, composed of the last strands of Mr. Jennings' hair, aroused in him strange primal stimulations & bio-electrical pangs. Upon his request one eve, I actually felt his quickened pulse coursing through his wrist. He sat back proudly, absorbed by the magnificence of his angel-winged Victorian chair, as if these exaggerated blips of pulse proved that he was something vaguely human afterall.

On the lining of the wig's skull cap is a small patch (I've seen it—I think), a miniature rendering of his Electric Chair litho series with the initials LDJ meticulously added to the back of the fateful electric chair.

Mr. Warhol never found a suitable replacement for Mr. Jennings, although he DID visit several other maximum security facilities in the early 80s. Mr. Jennings seemed to possess, for Mr. Warhol, that ideal confluence of victim & victimizer. The gruesome & spectacularly publicized proportions of his crime seemed to lend Mr. Jennings a certain Shakespearian mien, the appearance of a man of immense, if troubled, humanity. Mr. Warhol was, of course, always kept safely away from the ferocious & untidy details of Mr. Jennings' crimes.

On the aforementioned night, right after the General Vasectome Roast, I remember Mr. Warhol showing me his shaved morbid corpus, which more amused than aroused me. The side effects of massive injections of female hormones, scars where erectile tissue had been transplanted & all the scars from his 2 botched Mexican sex change operations had left him in a kind of quanderous ambi-sexual equilibrium, a kind of fleshy no-mans-land, which served only to mitigate any pleasure I might have been able to professionally squeeze out of the situation.

& as he tipped his head back in "Dying Slave" fashion in that posh angel-winged centaur-hooved Victorian chair, I saw his adam's apple bobbing up & down as he wearily whispered potentially lucrative insider trading information into my ear. As if it were no longer possible to fool himself that this numeric litany approximated the language God prefered. & then the wig fell off, like a bird's nest full of blue eggs. &, post-Harlow homage aside, his body went as rigid as a firm fish market bass on a bed of ice.

I have since dropped out of the competition to be "the Warhol that didn't really die." I don't have the stomach for the kind of intra-Factory spirit assassination it takes to be the someone I dread I really am anyway. (Besides, I don't have an agent. See *The Story of My Life*.)

But now, to put personal strife & further speculation aside, I must personally vouch for the location of that original "Freedom Power" wig. I assure you it is very safe in a Ziplock Baggie in a shoebox in the safe deposit box of a major east coast banking establishment.

I assure you I've gone to this safe deposit box & I've donned this wig for short intervals, but only within the very discreet confines of my private safe deposit cubicle. I prefer not to reveal the precise location of said wig at this time, for fear of involving you as possible accessories to this "crime." I hope that this recent Polaroid snapshot of said wig will satisfy any lingering doubts you may have. ▼

THE SUPPRESSION OF MIRTH

(NO LAUGHING MATTER)

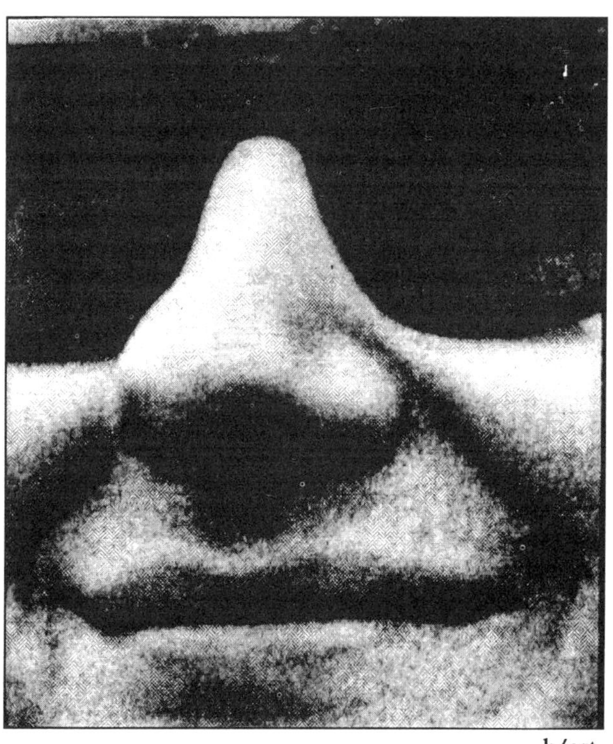

b/art

When the governed laugh, the governors cannot but have an uneasy feeling that they may be laughing at them.
• Malcolm Muggeridge

There has never been a consensus among nations regarding the nature of laughter. Many governments, including those of the former Eastern Bloc, do however, regard laughter as subversive & deleterious to social stability. & thus seek, each in their own way, if not a worldwide condemnation of laughter & its numerous parallel manifestations, then a national agenda to severely contain it.

Other governments, including the U.S.A. & those of Western Europe, regard much of the general spectrum of mirth as a variably effective form of mass control. As long as it stops shy of the "explosive & almost uncontrollable physical upheaval of the person," as Darwin once described it.

Politicians worldwide, meanwhile, are attempting to establish acceptable levels of mirth. Liberals favor a broad definition of what they're calling "harmless guffaws," thus enabling experts to pinpoint specific pernicious non-conformist laughter. But they agree, in principle, with hardline Lamenters that laughter should be employed in moderation. Caution, discretion, tolerance & charity should define the parameters of laughter. The remaining categories of acceptable mirth would be allowed to follow their course, inducing feelings of euphoria (based in consumption) & thus reinforcing the belief that everything is exactly as it should be.

However, along with the expansion of the Post-WWII middle class came the notion of attainable leisure as a reward for honest work. This class lived & worked not for power or beauty but for the consumption of their deserved comfort. The entertainment conglomerates arose to ply this burgeoning new class with a veritable non-stop laugh track of culture triumphant in leisure. It encouraged innocuous indulgence—banal laughter within socially prescribed parameters of accepted mirth, mirth that breaks up trains of thought & voids the possibilities for social change. Ultimately this creates a connection, ironically, between the universal acceptance of being a part of mankind while simultaneously encouraging the haughty, if petty ostentatious distinctions of a class that can afford leisure. Part of the mass, yet perceiving itself as somehow aloof from the masses.

Laughter has, since ancient times, been known as "nature's anxiety maintenance system." Herbert Spenser described it as an "overflow of nervous energy." Laughter is a prime socio-psychic curative in the maintenance of personal buoyancy & the management of the extreme absurdity of the modern world's complexities. "Laughter," for Emmanuel Kant, was thus, "an affection arising from the sudden transformation of a strained expectation into nothing." Even more to the point, William Hazlitt declared: "man is the only animal that laughs...for he is the only animal that is struck with the difference between what things are & what they ought to be."

It is in the need to distinguish between "positive" (civic/Vegas) & "negative" (subversive/Mirth Guerilla) laughter that governments are beginning to find room for agreement. First, positive laughter is beneficial laughter, laughter that reflects the society positively & affirms its values: family, work, religion, freedom within the parameters of consumerism. A propulsive factor in creating a society drugged on the consumption of well being.

Thus mirth beyond the officially sanctioned, the sort that might howl the house down, a laughter "of the whole man from head to heels," as Carlyle described it, is viewed as a laughter of subversion. "Mad laughter," a Dadaist "reaction against rigidity," becomes a weapon with which to resist & deconstruct the general oppressive regimentation of everyday life.

An accord, not dissimilar to the one condemning terrorism, currently being fleshed out would ease restrictions on humor in the post-Eastern Bloc, while the West would try to re-hone its definition of "positive laughter as socially uplifting"—instructive light rebuke, infirmities, social amenities & manners—the "lounge-style" of comedy. This strategy of comedy is based on the laugh track theory, a behaviorist form that trains people to laugh at certain junctures

& quips. Like advertising, it keeps the funny bone activated with no time to think.

A proposed cultural exchange would send many of America's "comic videos on the order of a dancing french fry," & situation comedies—*My Three Sons, The Brady Bunch, The Jeffersons, Three's Company, McHale's Navy, Father Knows Best, My Favorite Martian* & *The Munsters* (often disparagingly refered to by Mirth Guerillas as the "junk bonds of laughter")—to the former Eastern Bloc nations. The West would host the best of their court jesters, café comics & circus clowns. A proposed mixed card of Las Vegas-style stand up comics & the best of the East would tour the world: Moscow, Atlantic City, Sun City, Burbank, the Catskills, the Cote d'Azur.

Further agreement would create a network of cooperative surveillance to monitor & ultimately squelch the proliferation of laughter deemed anti-social. The focus appears aimed mainly at enclaves of volatile mirth-making. These habitués, or Mirth Guerillas, tend to hide in the relative anonymity of the world's larger metropolises. Target areas include Greenwich Village, New Orleans, Amsterdam, San Francisco, Rome, & Barcelona.

The estimated 2 million Bohemian Mirth Guerillas strive, according to the powerful Lament Lobby, "to Anarchist & Proto-Communal Euphoria schemes, exacerbating economic mayhem by circumventing government-sanctioned laughter, dealing in clandestine bartering, undermining the Mood Regulation Industry, hoping to ultimately toss Free Enterprise into utter disarray."

This notion of a guffaw gaggle of "anti-social low life scum" has been sharpened by the Lament Lobby, which insists laughter is prurient, like "spent spiritual effluvia," & umbilically attached to the sex organs. Thus restraint is a means for accumulating spiritual power. They believe the source of laughter is pan-demos—of the vulgar mob, the root of pandemonium (Aristotle called it turning the "world upside down"), the sacrilegious tool of anarchy. For them laughter's source is Greek comedy which delved into pagan rites of spring, copulation, wooden penises, pornographic sing-a-longs, Bacchanalian excess & unrepentent flatulence, which appears to jeopardize the progress of the soul.

Mega-Mood Conglomerates have already developed pills that promise to enhance feelings of patriotic euphoria (a sort of "red, white & blue X-tasy"), which appear to leave the work ethic fully intact. One pharmaceutical conglom claims development of caplets that utilize positive aspects of certain hallucinogens & amphetamines to produce a so-called "Puritan Opium," or P-OP.

In the other court, the Mirth Guerillas insist government-sanctioned levels of laughter enslave mankind to glum circumscribed moral, religious & aesthetic codes. Thus their "mad laughter," incorporating the anarchistic zest of the early Dadaists, is their "Harpo bouquet of squirting blossoms to the regiments of fanatical functionaries." In other words, laughter is spiritual combat.

But in the clown face of this growing international network of Mirth Guerillas one finds a vast mobilization of institutional resources created to set up methods to monitor laughter, proposing "decibel limits," licensing mirth emporiums & policing their proliferation through the development of ultra-sensitive sonar detection, Curlian photography & microwave monitoring. To go along with their developments of P-OP, the Mega-Mood Congloms have been recruited to develop an anti-febrile, counter-guffaw innoculation for the masses.

Ultra-Lamenters believe that "a patriotic grin is just as effective without the demonstrative vulgarity," & propose herding all overt expressions of mirth into an annual holiday for "mirth letting." Perhaps one tied into the New Year's, St. Patrick's or Mardi Gras celebrations? While some anti-mirth monetarists, worried about the erosion of the work ethic, propose tying the "mirth-rate" to a work-inducement regressive tax-scale, where wealth & workaholism would be rewarded with certain "mirth credits." These ultra-Lamenters seem fond of anachronistic notions of station & caste, hearkening back to times when mirth was the sole privilege of royalty & the well-rested.

The Moral Militia (MM), a Lament Lobby-funded research group, has manufactured "incontrovertible evidence that Jesus never laughed." What ennobled him as the Son of God, they claim, was that he was capable of laughing but CHOSE not to. This notion informs the very foundation upon which they've built a prolific dissemination network. Their Moral Militia Media Center (3M) in Hooeyville, West Virginia, contends the Bible reveals "inexorable connections between glee, psychopathic behavior, abuses of freedom & the decay of our most cherished values."

They've recently released a study of computer-enhanced news photos which is fast becoming a litmus test for the socially-acceptable limits of mirth. It is a controversial condemnation of laughter which attempts to show incontrovertible connections between avid smiling & some of this century's most notorious personages. Three key sociopaths they studied are "Squeaky" Fromme of the Charles Manson clan, a purported unrepentent laugher—even after her assassination attempt on President Ford. They also looked at Arthur "Savage Smile" Bremer & David "Smirk of Sam" Berkowitz. Bremer's quasi-euphoric smile has on the other hand, ironically been likened by the Mirth Guerillas to the heavenly god-inspired smile of the Pope, whose holy smiles are, of course, exempt from regulation. Herein, the MM maintains, lies the imminent danger: an effort on the part of Mirth Guerillas in concert with renowned sociopaths seeking to obliterate the distinctions between good & "mad laughter" & "hoodwinking the masses & destroying their moral fiber & inalienable rights to consume."

Hitler, the MM has oft pointed out, was also a fanatical smirker, ennabling him to beguile a whole continent with his infectious "gest pucker." But the Mirth Guerillas point out that Hitler, like kings, presidents & CEOs before & after him, employed a systemmatic method for squelching all ridiculing laughter. The cruel facts of his secret persecution & ultimate extermination of all those deemed guilty of *"offenbare gefährliche Gelachter"* (obviously dangerous laughter) has only recently come to light.

The MM's report also states that Charles Manson held Jack the Ripper's smile in high regard. In fact, he was obsessed with its Devilish power. Manson apparently often held 3-day smile sessions & incantatory cackling rites to develop "the dark powers of mockery & smuggery." Thus, they contend, laughter needs stricter regulation because it "lifts the veil of regret, remorse & social morés, triggering feelings of expansive amorality, which is, afterall, the Devil's Playground."

The MM, with tacit U.S. Government approval, has joined its former Cold War adversaries, the agents of Perpetual Sullenness at the Kremlin. These foot soldiers of dreariness have mobilized posses to penetrate the hotbeds of mirth. They recommend the picketing & re-zoning of areas known as the breeding grounds for that malicious brand of "mad laughter & jubilant iniquity." Their plan of attack also calls for disruption, hooliganism, preferential treatment, reverse quota systems, withholding of legitimate promotions & raises, photo-documentation, context humiliation, blackmail & agent provocateurs.

The zealous 3M claims most Mirth Guerillas tend to be "Jewish, black, homo, bi- or asexual, liberal to leftist with smatterings of anarchists, humanists, pacifists & neo-Dadaists—the W.C. Fields-Lenny Bruce-Marx Brothers-Ernie Kovacs-Krazy Kat orgiastic axis that seeks to overthrow the inalienable rights of those who live under the law of God & Government."

Young Anti-Mirth Soldiers (Y.A.M.S.) recently attacked the editorial offices of college satire magazines that ridicule institutions. *The Harvard Lampoon* has been hard hit by pooperscooper-toting YAMS who hurl feces from frat house catapults. *Mad, Weirdo & Screw* have been shoplifted or mysteriously ignited on newstands. Distributors balk because, although many may believe in freedom of the press, they say their liability insurance rates have skyrocketed.

So, ironically enough, post-Hitlerian homilies like "Work will set you free" have found their way into popular advertising campaigns.

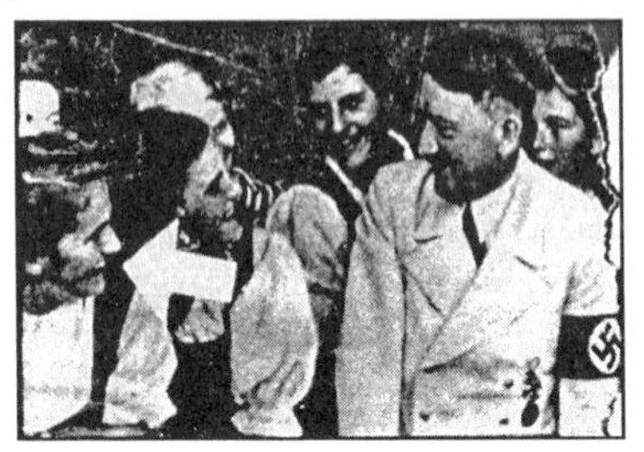

Coca Cola has led the way with: "COKE WORKS FOR YOUR PLEASURE." McDonald's: "AFTER A HARD DAY'S WORK, BE A BIG MAC KING & LET US WAIT ON YOU." Levi's: "JEANS THAT WORK HARD TO MAKE YOU A BETTER-LOOKIN' WORKER."

Self-help TV therapists for chronic chucklers & unrepentent gigglers have popped up all over America. Even the drug problem has been attributed to a "mutually parasitic" source of blatant anti-social laughter.

One hears gruesome tales of mirth-addicts laughing themselves to death. Public service messages, in the style of *Reefer Madness,* relate typical laughter-related tragedies. The stories emphasize such clichés as gallows humor, splitting one's sides, burst with laughter, die laughing to create the intimate & undeniable connection between laughter & death. Emphasizing techniques developed by anti-drug campaigns, they warn of comedy troupes weaving evil hallucinatory spells of ribald aspersions & insidious wackiness to produce rollicking types of involuntary laughter. Hypnotized by the black humor, audiences collapse into "tear the whole house down" chaos!

The MM, with seemingly unlimited funds & media access, is determined to create connections between laughter & every social ill—aetheism, masturbation, incest, alcoholism, overeating, the high incidence of "mirth infection" (contact highs), "a chain reaction of cerebral anarchy where credit cards, logic, carnivores & family life

are trashed through chortling as well as an unfeeling, brash disregard for humanity." Henri Bergson, a frequent source for the 3M, said that a necessary condition of laughter is an absence of feeling, "for laughter has no greater foe than emotion."

Ulrike Meinhof was a tittering terrorist in another vein. Her tragedy (she died in prison awaiting trial; some claim she used derisive laughter against her captors & this led to her being suspiciously "suicided") is portrayed by the 3M as an "attraction to the deceptive liberating qualities of laughter." Her *Authoritative Compendium Of The Suppression Of Laughter From The Middle Ages To The Modern Age* is often cited by Mirth Guerillas. Her acts in the name of emancipation led to the first worldwide crackdowns on flagrant mirthers.

It's safe to say that today we are in the midst of a worldwide struggle for the funnybone of humanity. The extreme MM issues solemn decrees of puritanical mirthocalypse, & governments favor some restrictions on "mad laughter," while the international "cabal" of Mirth Guerillas & Liberation Mirth Monks ("God laughed 7 times to create the world: the first laugh to create light; the second created water;...the seventh laugh bore the soul.") believe that laughter emancipates body & soul from the tyranny of the mundane & temporal. ▼

WET DREAMS OF THE POPE

(written as a collaboration with Black Sifichi)

Valerie Haller

> *The psychoanalytical theory of money must start by establishing the proposition that money is, in Shakespeare's words, the 'visible god'; in Luther's words, 'the God of this world.'*
> **• Norman O. Brown**

ONE

It always begins the same way. The same way for the Pope. The same white meat. White-Oh-Glory-Be tender flesh. Nautical reveries in white chaussettes. Stretched *rêves* of whispered white across sharp delicate ankle bones. Bones worthy of any religion or reliquary.

The Pope has discovered her ankles to be deserving of embracement & adulation. & he has in his mind already traced the rivulets of perspiration she has imported from her Venice with the velvet piping of his sleeve. Her ankles are indeed worthy of praise because they are grace inside flesh & of fantastic manufacture: brittle, precise, bird-like.

He is attuned to these delights (although, for propriety's sake he will never reveal the nausea that craving causes in his solar plexus) because, afterall, had this Pope not once been a poet? Thus, does it not seem likely that he, in the course of his writings, would have traversed the tight inseams, that hem of the Him & Her, where flesh is forever chainstitched to reverie? The prevailing notion of poetry, which seems to contain freedom in it somewhere, would seem to make all these questions foregone conclusions.

& what of her bellbottoms? Are they not always pink, pink & diaphanous? Like a gondola made of rose petals. Tight & pink as stipulated. Pink & as provocative as a smile floating by on the canals of her Venice. Pink as an unhealed wound of lilies on the ponds of Giverney. & was it not this gorgeous pink (beautiful as a heretic's tongue kiss) that provoked him to imagine her as exquisite *flora rosa*? As something pink & aromatic. Floating & hinged. Slang & seminal. Pink & carnivorous.

TWO

But it always leads to this same place. Like dog to same tree, blessing with his urine the fallen leaves which will eventually blow away, disappear, ashes to ashes, dust to dust. Only the *parfum* will linger, invisible, like a saint, or spirit, like an undiscovered apse containing the delicate pink marble statue of the Virgin Mary, "Pink & Carnivorous." The scent wafts among the listing taxis along the dark *Fume Della Pieta* like incense down the nave of a glass cathedral, slithering ichthyo-fishily through subterranean channels. Until suddenly...light, gold, sun, huge open sky, purple waters shimmering.

Shimmering vulvic gondola. Images triggered by neuron, ganglion & solar plexis, leaning over & dragging his hand through the diaphonous fluid. The gondolier guides the vessel into the *Bacino Di San Marco*. San Marco's *torre* rises in the near distance. The sensation between departure and arrival dances like bullets in the Pope's chest. He knows the feel of the hot bullet, the miracle of bulletproof glass, the difference between speed & impact, flame & gypsy moth.

The papal colours change at *Canal Vallaresso*. The terra firma hues of the *torre* bricks add a sense of earthly stability to which the Pope responds. The combination of the way her curves round harmoniously into the echo of the Byzantine *arco*, with its muscular knots of stone; the way her silence fits perfectly into the pews of Saint Peter's, perfect for vigilance & circumspection, & the way her delicate moiré-scaled pale hands wave wistfully; all seem to mirror his own gestures, giving eternal value to vision & dream.

She looks down as his gondola nudges the piles into its snug berth. He's like a lost sailor, a *marinaio* dressed in white cope heavy with knuckles of jewelry, delivered before his *sirena*. Hoping she will bless him with extraordinary knowledge, with the wetness of rutting season, recovery, bottomless breath & the amphibious freedom of multi-dimensional movement. Not just Forward & Back, To & Fro, In & Out, but forever Through & Within, Above & Below, Confessor & Confessed, the unity of a circle with the balance of a cube.

The gondola dipped unsteadily as the gondolier leapt to the pier with the aid of his *remo,* long elegant oar of gondoliers, near the *Teatro San Moise.* A book drops from his striped jacket pocket—William Pope's *HOLYSTONE* falls open at page 111. The Pope reads:

> *I have done the damnable deed. The horrible damnable deed. I cannot pray. God will have nothing to do with me. I will not have salvation at his hands. I long to be in the bottomless pit, the lake which burneth with fire and brimstone ... Oh God, do not hear my prayers for I will not be saved. I hate everything that God has made.*

He hands the book back to his gondolier, & looks up at the tower. She's no longer there. He wonders if Mr. Pope's text would still be valid if he substituted the word "salvation" with "orgasm"—as in I will not have orgasm. Unforgettable speculations that only the courtesan-rife floating history of Venezia could adequately provide. The same Venezia that has sullied its own canals as well as our collective lyricism. The same Venezia that now looked more like a rundown Luna Park de Pizzas, along the Merceria, with its dealers of plastic gondolas made in China. The same Venezia which back in 1562 decreed all gondolas be black because they had become objects of ostentacious display. But was the gondola not now the perfect container for her white & pink servitudes?

The gondolier continued with his book. The Pope wiped sweat from brow. Kept a 3rd eye on the tower for some sign of his bellbottomed "Bovolo." But she had taken a simple step back (had vacated) into the sanctity of shadow, perhaps too cool to indulge in secret sentimentalities, however utilitarian. The gondolier glanced up too, curious as to the object of the Pope's gaze. He paused an instant & then asked into the empty *trompe l'oeil* space, "Is money God in action, *Dio di Dollaro,* Your Holiness?"

THREE

Perhaps the Pope had been too obstinate to insist that Money could NEVER (as in Absolutely Not Ever) be God in action. [In 1955 the U.S. Congress even passed a law requiring that ALL U.S. coins & paper money carry the motto, In God We Trust.] Just as likely, though, the Pope (official title: Bishop of Rome, Vicar of Jesus Christ, Successor of the Prince of the Apostles, Supreme Pontiff of the Universal Church, Patriarch of the West, Primate of Italy, Archbishop & Metropolitan of the Roman Province & Sovereign of the *Stato Della Citta Del Vaticano*) had allowed critical acumen to succumb to the assembled belief in his de facto moral & spiritual infallibility.

To admit on any level that *Dio* on occasion could be Money in action was tantamount to admitting that he was nothing more than a ridiculously overdressed bankteller. But to get back to the point, which is power, there was no point in the Pope denying the facts of his vast temporal powers. The Pope was, afterall, the director of such important functions as the manufacture of the Vatican's postage stamps, coins, flags, & license plates, as well as the operation of the Vatican's (i.e. HIS) own telecommunications system, radio station & *banca*.

Perhaps at some juncture the Pope had stopped asking for divine assistance, as the successor of St. Peter, in matters both spiritual & temporal? Perhaps he'd lost his bearings? Perhaps he'd begun to rely too much on financial alchemists such as Michel Sindona? Perhaps politics had left him without the courage or wherewithal to admit certain truths? We, of course, have no way of knowing any of this.

But perhaps the belief (for what is belief but just a more desperately certified hope?), by Roman Catholics that Christ established the Vatican when he said: "Upon this rock I will build my Church...", by extrapolation, came to mean the Pontiff was infallible. Which led him to affect a certain Papal swagger, a certain magnificent & cinematic toss of his sumptuous white wool-banded vestments which made his cape ripple with all the aplomb of a matador who defies death the way a Pope must defy doubt & temptation.

Actually, the Pope stood to gain much by denying the very immensity of these temporal powers. This denial—no matter how elegant or articulate—had long ago become an inverted form of bragadosio, the hubris of over-invoked humility. He can kiss earth or viscous pavement or a leper's gnarled forehead a thousand times & it will still be not unlike a gigolo in baggy pants refusing to call attention to the bulk of his bulge.

Thus his immense temporal power is ultimately enhanced by the assertive pomposity of his denials. &, in spite of all his obstinancy, had he not already bought her? Or tried to? Had he not already decided that money was no object? Yes, he had indeed paid her train fare to HIS Rome from HER Venice, the Venice of Proust, Casanova & Mann, where during Carnivale, just a week ago, he had experienced the magical, warm southeasterly Scirocco bluster down narrow *callis*, rippling the water on the *rii*, surprising the souls of some & the skins of others. In fact, this Scirocco had done much more. It had lifted the intimate, overlapping cycloid scales off of her fabulous bombastic fusiform; flapping gently like spangles on the sigh of a summer dress.

Yes, he had sensed that his magniloquently-informed *vista guidata* of private Vatican treasures, made of ivory, gold & geld would impress her. He had thought that his well-timed pious & sweeping hand gestures, revealing priceless (too expensive for a mortal to conceive) statuary, Egyptian & Etruscan antiquities & gilt (beyond guilt?) framed oils would leave her in his thrall.

But instead, she was awed more by how easily she had gained his confidence, by how obediently he had donned a particular pair of jeans. The knees of these jeans were already chalky because he had already been down on his knees before her furlocked *amoretto gusto* sandals (based on the design of a certain slender *vaporetto*) & had already impetuously bludgeoned her with flattery, likening her to a breathless Venus; an Ingres on fire; a torrid Titian with "the lazy caterpillar brows wrapped around aromatic cup-of-coffee eyes." She forgave him his purple poetics.

Hymn \ him \ n [ME *ymne,* fr. OF fr. L *hymnus* song of praise, fr. Gk *hymnos*] 1: a song of praise 2: a song of joy. hyomen \ hiomen \ n [LL, fr. Gk *hymen* membrane]: a fold of mucous membrane partly closing the orifice of the vagina—Hymen [L, fr. Gk *Hymen*]: the Greek god of marriage.

The Pope was emboldened by what he read in the dictionary. It convinced him that hymen contained "hi men!"—a greeting, a welcome, an invitation. & that hymn sounded like him & that both hymn & hymen were marked by God as part of their meaning. This gave the Pope a better sense of his Manifest Destiny, that his future with her was not only inevitable but expansive & benevolent as well.

But she remained curiously in & of herself. That is to say, untouchable. That is to say numinous. Illuminous. Unreproachable, unapproachable. Like inexplicable points of light in the sky.

On his knees the loose change of many nations jiggled in his pockets. Before her he was both nervy & nervous. He confessed that he liked the snug fit of the jeans, the way they clung to his loins, as she'd predicted. & he caressed his own hips & loins in much the same manner that John Travolta had in a previous, more incendiary incarnation. Had the Pope studied Travolta's gestures, or were they mere genetically coded movements that informed the male species of the gestural ritual of courtship? No matter.

For it was the Pope who controlled a massive Holy Empire, with 800 million adherents prepared to believe his every infallible utterance. He knew she'd denounced her faith, knew that he could ceremoniously forgive her & gain political leverage. He knew she'd done time for seditious acts, in the women's prison on the *Isola* of Giudecca in a previous incarnation. & he knew that she knew what he knew. & yet, somehow he was NOT in control. In fact, the more faraway her eyes seemed the more he sensed she could see right through him.

She had already remarked that the way he looked in jeans pleased her. & he had already blushed red, a blood-engorged red, the same red as his shoes, the ones with crosses embroidered on the front.

She had already issued her derisive laugh, noting that the 2 chalky spots on his knees resembled his bald spot. & she had already sardonically made the sign of the cross, touching each of his 3 "bald stigmata" in proper sequence. It was gestures of this sort that made him realize he could never again leave her alone. That he could never let her leave. That she could never leave this Palace of 1000 rooms alone—or alive.

He must discover within himself a way to convince her that HE was curator & SHE mere bauble. That HE was sculptor & SHE his voluptuously contoured statuary. & he must assure her that his *banca* was always open, that money was of no value, that by showering her with it he would prove her more valued than all the In God We Trust dollars, yen or marks in his bank.

& ultimately he knew this woman (thought he knew the soul of Woman), that this would impress her & ultimately yank down her sardonic guard. He thinks this will prop up his charade which can best be described as that pious swagger.

But before HER he is always humble (but only in as much as he thinks this will manipulate her)—& alone. & all else is *merde*. & he thinks this well-rehearsed humility (which is nothing but well-dressed unrequited yearning) will impress her. & if not impress her, confuse her. But he could NOT have been more wrong.

FOUR

Confused she was not & impressed she only pretended to be. She had lived in Paris, eating with the bourgeoisie, hobnobbing with ministers of business & culture as a translator for a large multi-national based in Rome. Quick talk, hollow promises & exhorbitant, tax-subsidized meals were old barbeques for her.

She was well-accustomed to her own beauty. She wore it like a short strapless sequined dress on a starry night, exciting all with the gravity & brilliance she could only see indirectly via the reflections in the eyes of her wrought-up suitors. Eyes that shimmered relative to the amount of "shimmy" she decided to generate. Eyes like thermometers. Beauty as barometer. She controlled the climate. & all this getting to know the wealthy was mere prep for meeting the Pope, whose ties to organized crime & multi-nats she did not underestimate.

She was prepared, prepared for his being prepared. But he wasn't. While the Pope was lost in the blue cling of his new Levi's (deliriously noting the anagram of which spelled ELVIS/EVILS), she had already begun her assault. She had already crossed the thresh-hold of propriety when she'd passed behind a "delicious" Michelangelo & unbuttoned a blouse button.

He hadn't noticed her pass behind the statue. But when she reappeared he did notice the undone button (like the wink of a whore). After the button—the undone. After the undone—the hole. After hole—gold Cross. Gold Cross above her *poitrine. Feditura exotica* under Cross. Cross near the hole.

"Which came first?" He mused. "Button or Cross? Chicken or egg? Passion or passion flower? Poem or poet?"

His Holiness wrote in a vision:
Virginal Vesuvian Firsts
Holy Primary Hymens
Singular Secular Penetrations
Unique Mysterious Union
Infinite Unending Intercourse

The Pope had his Roman way with Latin phonics & allusion, despite his Eastern European background. & this poetry, this 1st poem of the day, this unwritten sketch which had almost alighted from his lips (the translation could reach millions) he wanted to first transcribe into Kinetics. Kinetics with her. Vowel into skin touch. Consonants into grunts & cries. Verb into crevice. Thrust, heave, torque.

"All good things in time," she purred, the words coming from on high, descending through her from some far off place to finish his thought. Like the host finished communion. He mused. If the body of Christ can transport itself as a salty wafer...could he not be transported by trucks carrying sweet biscuits in the shape of the Virgin Mary's nipples? *Popo Biscotto!* "The Mother & Son in One."

The Pope's mind was ablaze with new ideas, sensations, marketing plans & sexual allegories. Bovolo was source to amazing inspirations, not triggered by daily routine, but by the grandiose, the global, satellites, private *musées*. Close things—open buttons. Feminine things. The Pope needed special things to excite him. Long distance phone sex. But why call when he could be live?

& so he journeyed to Venice, home of his predecessor, John Paul I (a sentimental aescetic, romantic Luddite, heretic, loony lacking the proper grandeur, he smugly judged). & while visiting the newly restored paintings in the *Chiese San Marco,* he had captured one of the most beautiful women in Italy, utilizing twinkle in eye, a Brando lisp in 12 languages, video tapes of himself in passionate arousal before 25,000 Byelorussians & Lithuanians in Lomza, his 5000 press-books, 100 bank accounts, 1900kw of radio power, his *immobilier* on the Champs Elysees, & Vatican tourist profits (4120 visitors daily).

The figures seemed to swoon her like the image of the Milky Way, or all the galaxies in the universe, or the square of the square of the square.

"My cubic presence is probably the greatest of any individual on the planet," he proclaimed with a smile. But while he was remembering & multiplying "worldly things," (millions invested in dummy bonds, guns, bombs, tanks, speculative ventures, real estate, even contraceptives) another button opened to reveal yet another hole. And near this hole he spotted a fold of flesh. Powdery cool bronzed *pelle* (as cultivated on the Lido). Orbital flesh. Buttonhole flesh.

His conquest wandered through the gallery, pausing at statuary, observing paintings, touching velvet draperies. Elusive, at arm's breath. All while appearing to be warm(?)...provocative(?)

&...just...just...barely...stripping.

The Pope slipped in & out of himself, the warp & woof of ecstasy & fact, as Bovolo pushed hands into pockets, feeling her own loins, breathing, just 10 feet ahead in a farflung corner of his vision. & his jeans revealed what his robes had always concealed: the curve of his excitement had begun to pulsate. & the darkness of the gallery scythed out a swath of freedom (that freedom & darkness were symbiotically connected was, at best, an excommunicable notion). In the dark all humility & guilt evaporated. Its brumal clime donated a "rational temperature"—680F, 170C, the temp. of invigoration & arousal—where temporal & physical were "perfectly balanced." Even if the pendulous profundity of his testicular globosity was lost.

He sat like a male model for a sexy yoghurt ad, one leg up on a crate, other dangling, his sex centered & forward. The gilt-framed art provided him a spine of comfort, & the Pope felt good. Rich but somehow Bohemian. His sinewy nerves revealed themselves to be as functional as dense fiberoptic cables. The kind laid along the ocean's floor. & then—flash frames: Dark-lit forest scenes; Paintings of the hunt; Titian's *Rape of Europa*.

& with a swing of his scepter & a valiant lunge mid-groin she became living sculpture to add to his vast collection. Or the Vatican Arboretum. Or Zoo?! Crown her "Queen Bee Pope Joan;" or, "Anti-Pope of Avignon," or "*Femme Sovereigna di Zen Button.*" In tiara & bikini of her choice. Would his Polish poetry, with its gutteral incantations, convince her to partake of such a venture?

The Pope continued to slip between quandry & reverie, while she orbited about him playing her cool game of Duchampian "chess." "Chess with a razor," was a phrase that came often to mind. And this "razor" she imagined with ivory handle, ergonomically sculpted for a Botticelli hand, supporting silver blade, fired black, gleaming, one edge a French curve the other as straight as an assassin's bullet.

It is with this mental blade that she starts to "play." It is with this mental blade that she intends to "castrate" the Pope, pry open "locks" of information, "engrave" her initials on the bedposts of the king size bed she imagines awaits them.

PLAY CASTRATE LOCK ENGRAVE.

The holes that normally held buttons in place were now beginning to hold the Pope in place. "My kingdom for another undone button," she mumbled sarcastically, regarding the bulge he tried to hide with his white ecclesiastical beret.

She had been quiet long enough & thus she entered the middle game. Strop the razor; make her seemingly defensive position, fait accompli, offensive & undeniable. Yet she had to sustain a sexual gravity more magnetic than self-same blade &, eventually, swing back & slice his desire to holysmoke.

A magnetic storm of the highest order. Lightning. Gleam of blade. Thunder. Tornado of tug & torque. Echoes of stabbings. Shower of confessed tears. Blood. Ink of Royal Colour. She demanded the secret 10 *Comandamentos* written by Pope Pie XI, after he'd met with Marinetti & the other Futurists in the Vatican to put forth their theories of man & machine.

After the death of Pie XI in 1939, war broke out & these *Comandamentos* were deemed too sacred to be read by anyone save successive Popes.

Bovolo was also interested in the *3 Letters of The Fatima*; Nostradamus' unpublished writing, cribbed by Hitler; Caesar's litanies on Hypnotism & Power; The *Quanta Cura* (in which the Papacy denounced the notions of unrestricted liberty & aligned itself with juntas & absolute monarchies); secret records of the *Istituto per le Opere di Religione;* or IOR; or Vatican Bank; the AIDS File; the unedited tapes of John Paul I speeches; books on Erotica; the Index *Librorum Prohibitorum* of banned books & diaries kept by country priests on exotic isles.

She undid a 3rd button. The Pope eyed lace. Black lace. Plunging neckline. Gravity made stronger by the insinuation of bosom. He wanted to examine the manufacture of her brasierre, a lace *reggipeto*, when suddenly she sparked up. "Was it a sexual fantasy that killed John Paul I?" Long pause. "Or was he poisoned with digitalis, which neatly simulates a myocardial infarcation—for having refused to wear the Papal Crown?"

She leaned back, nipples pressing through her pink silk blouse. He knew so much, but every instant there was more he would never fathom.

Mouth agape, legs spread & flexed, *prêt à commencer,* he felt domination, something cinematic, something culturally ordained. She sauntered over to him, epic arching eyes fixed to his, lips pursed *Vogue*-style. But before he could speak she cut him again, this time with a demand. "Let's have the secret *Comandamentos,* Your Holiness!'

The Pope lost his tongue for all 12 languages. Fixed his stare on the next undone button. He knew he'd tell her. His silence already ample confession. Compliance. Hypnotic acquiescence.

She leaned over, put her hands on his flexed knees. He felt like a crab on its back. His beret fell to the floor & she let out a "MMM-MMMM"—somewhere between mantra & gastronomic delight. He stared down the flagrant *feditura* V, her blouse open to navel. "Well," she taunted, stood up, rubbed the last button (& his imagination) between her fingers, "Show me the book."

He stood up. Hair on end. In the adjacent hallway lined with Fra Angelicos, Pinturiccios, & Raphaels they entered a small closet which contained a locked door. Here he matted his frightwig with sweat & spit. Secret closets led to secret bowers & more locked doors. The Pope punched in a code & the next door opened. Inside, a small staircase spiralled up 2 flights to another electronically locked door.

"The library," he said as he winked & tapped in the code. Click. Open. Shuffle. Click. Stolen embrace. Closed. Furtive sigh. The Pope opened a small light at a reading desk. An immense library. "31,000 Ancient Latin manuscripts. 400,000 books. This inner sanctum houses some of the world's most valued tomes."

"Sit down, relax," she said as she surveyed the shelves, fingering leather spines, calling out titles & catalogue numbers.

"#8666," he shouted. "Over to the right." She quickly found her way & slid out a Gold & Black codex with PIE XI engraved inside the Golden Papal Bull. She took the book to his table where her blouse unfolded like the limp petals of a chrysanthemum. Her semi-erect nipples mesmerized him.

"Have you read this?"

"Of course," he answered dryly, his perineum like a lit fuse. "I could've recited it to you, but knew you wouldn't accept it without seeing it with your own eyes." She gazed down at the unopened tome & then back at him. The game listed to & fro, but ever forward. This sudden candor on his part...was it naiveté? Good heartedness? Trust? How sharp was he? His vanity had (the faithful were relieved to learn), after John Paul I's embarassing charade of trashy humility, reasserted its earthly duty of manifesting God's prowess with a vengence.

"Recitez, s'il vous plait."

The Pope closed his eyes & spoke as if from a trance, as if each commandment would roll around one's mind the way her root beer sweet meat nipples might roll around in one's mouth.

10 *COMANDAMENTOS* FOR PARADISE ON EARTH:

1. Attach yourself to nothing. Live dangerously but not foolishly. Laugh in the face of authority.
2. Regard nothing as being higher than Yourself. Walk the Earth for 7 consecutive sleepless days & claim Yourself as creator.
3. Love thy neighbor ephemerally, unconsciously & lustfully. Let no image be prohibited to the speed of imagination.
4. The imagination is as large as the universe. Let it proliferate.
5. Let no ONE vice control You. Instead, let several compete simultaneously. Nothing is more simple than a singleviced man.

6. Pleasure of the flesh should rise with You every morning. Ponder its immensity, its poetry, its form; touch all roundness, fill all slips in space, fertilize all unlaid eggs.
7. Be rich & richer in Your generosity. Wealth has no definition if there are poor nearby.
8. All is natural: Cars, Earth, Bombs, Flowers. Embrace all & instill each in its proper place. Power has no definition if not compared to beauty.
9. Influence many. A sound idea should be heard by all. Walk the streets talking loud, stand on boxes & shout, if you have access to vision find a microphone, hire a stadium.
10. Be afraid of no one. Invite all types of experience. Fear has no relevance when its source is multiplied by the speed of light.

The Pope sat silent. Bovolo, with opened tome, verified the text. Accurate to the word. A chill fluttered down her spine.

FIVE

& how do you know when you know too much? Is it the chill breeze that stirs the vain in weathervane? In the 5th Century the Latin Cross made its first appearance on the tomb of an empress. Would he say she looked like that empress? Ben Her? For effect? For leverage? She hoped not.

Wasn't his capo swagger in snazzy low-brimmed lynx fedora not unlike that of a 2-shit, sloshed gambler on a lucky tear? Proud as any trucker parking his 18 wheels on a narrow Roman street during rush hour? But none of this was the issue.

He tried to amuse her with an ivory back scratcher, in the shape of a Latin cross, a gift from Mozambique. At each point of the cross sat a small, flexed hand ready to scratch where itches might crawl. "*Ta una pelle morbida.*" Her skin was indeed soft.

"*Arrêt* already!" She had to think fast, straight, solid & expansively, like a small caliber bullet that causes big damage. "You & your support for *Humanae Vitae* & the shabby *triste* treatment of women."

"Mary, Our Mother of God, yes, was not among the Apostles at the Last supper. No?"

The outline of inquiry, observation & incredulity looked like this: Papal intrusion #1: "Christ was first shown crucified on the cross in the 11th Century. The cross is also central to the Mandala. The cross divides mandala into quadrants, each arm represents a cardinal point. Christ's head was placed in the orb of the sun at the exact intersection of the arms of the cross."

"*Viva il Papa!*" she proclaimed with playful scorn. "& what of Calvi's head?"

1. Again, was he merely proud of his photographic memory? As much as he was, say, of his photogenic majesty?

2. Was he REALLY totally oblivious to the heretical nature of his peculiar 10 Commandments? Or, for that matter, the gunrunning, money laundering, blackmail, hoodlum accounts & arming of pro-Christian juntas.

3. Or was he letting her in on some Grand Secret, a hidden agenda? Apart from, or integral to, the very future of Catholicism? She thought not. Concentrations of power cannot withstand such notions as "laughing in the face of authority."

These Commandments would merely empower those who had never before been empowered. & in the eyes of Catholic Curia, this couldn't be anything but foolishly heretical. Because power would no longer be power if it could no longer hurt the many for the aggrandizement of the few.

Papal Intrusion #2: (Strategy; the glamour of humility placed, in his person, at her feet, to consolidate power. I.e. flattery amply applied will get you EVERYwhere.) Thus he is upon his knees before her. & here he unties her *chaussure* of missing leather, her furlocked *amoretto gusto* sandal, & he re-ties it too tight. Just right. He runs his tongue along the fleshy hints & along the stitches to count them, & bless their ample constrictiveness.

(From Vedic documents one learns that the cross [also the swastika, by the way] is related to their Fire Cult. Both the Cross & Fire Cult refer to pieces of wood necessary to make fire. & fire here is symbolic of the divine spark as represented by the sun. Sympathetic magic to renew the sun daily at dawn. The ceremony of burning the lamb corresponds with Jewish Passover traditions in which 2 spits were driven through the victim to form a cross. Christ's sacrifice on the cross took place during this same festival of the Vernal Equinox. Jung finds in this symbolism a key to tracing the liberation of libido for cultural creativity...)

4. Was he prepared to admit Christianity had merely been cribbed from Jewish & pagan rites, & was, in effect, a copycat religion?

4a. Was he prepared to come clean with the "facts"? During WWII some Vatican nuns did stow Jews away from the Nazis. Many others sheltered Nazis from the clutches of advancing Allies, & eventually affected their escapes to Argentina & Bolivia? & Vatican Inc. money, through P2, funded death squads & private Neo-Nazi armies in South America.

5. Was his heretical 10-Commandment mumbo jumbo meant to appease her? Make her believe he was some kind of Papal Blue Gene Vincent? Was all this pagan stuff just meant to get inside her pink bells? Or inside her blue *aide-memoire*?

6. Was he merely needling her because he knew she was a member of Venezia's branch of A/rivista Anarchica (for whom she'd done time, martyred by the *sub-terre* press as a more astute & sexier Ulrike Meinhof?)

7. Did he realize how close to Anarchist theory his 10 Commandments sounded? Did he believe its premises? Or only in so much as it could spook her? Afterall, hadn't he rescinded all support for the Medellin Manifesto, drafted by liberation theologists? & wasn't he a proponent of The Canon Law of Marriage (which believed in 3 criteria for marriage: erection, ejaculation, conception—a total rejection of pleasure & oral contraception?)

8. How much of his gunslinging bragadosio regarding the Vati-

can's intricate citizen surveillance network, modelled on South Africa's, was true? Was it REALLY called "The Eye Of God"?

Papal Intrusion #3: "Earthly prison of anima," he remarked as he held her foot enshrined in sandal. "I know how you wear out your heels in this unusual manner." He boasted. "The Great Shoemaker knows. The Church rejects atheists but respects them as creatures of God." He winked.

"As long as they're creatures in a cage," she countered. & he tied the laces of her left sandal tight too, & dreamt he had the power to hurt her—to hurt arch, bridge, knee, back of neck with the weighted cudgel of ivory wrapped in zebra hide he hid in a secret *poche* in the folds of his vestments. He watched her traipse & hobble, confident of the secret pain & its preachments, & hoped he'd always control her walk this way, & not that her walk might control him.

(The protective enclosure of the mandala is displayed during meditation. Outer circle full of fire. Flame of desire, your Venezia, your *Parigi, Nuovo York*. Unclean streets, burning genitalia burning with disease.)

To get his sleeping limbs moving, their blood circulating, he urged her over to the ancient lead glass window with its warped view of the meticulously kept *giardino* which purportedly mirrored the notions of the mandala.

"Our gardener sometimes pinches the blossoms before their bloom is totally spent. He does so because no one tells him otherwise. The Garden of Eden is the world's most famous contemplative enclosure. There stands the Tree of Life, cosmic beech, axis of the entire spiritual universe. Over there." He pointed, breathing into her nape. His breath hot & smelling of radishes. "It marks where many Christians were martyred in Nero's gardens. Here you will dwell & become familiar with its flora. Here you will be freed of your delusive knowledge, become child of nature, libertine of earthly & divine process."

"Cut the *merde* Baldhead! It's like Disney meets the Bible as done by Frank Capra. I know what gives & who takes what behind the bronze doors of the Basilica, past those snoozing Swiss guards in bumble bee pantaloons."

"This flower garden of the philosophers..."

"Junkyard of money launderers, sniper theologians, land speculators & hitmen for God."

"One can't run a church on Hail Marys."

"Nor, *Cor Unum,* alms collected supposedly, haha, for the poor."

"What you think you know you really don't. The doors to all banks open to the Right, my lil fish sandwich."

She glared at him, bit her lower lip.

"Blessed are the poor—& of course those who convince me of their worth," he said, with his 3-tier beehive tiara encrusted with precious stones, tilted rakishly across his dashing eyes.

"Enough mumbo sophistry. Cut the jive!"

"There is the contemplation pond with Monet lilies. Here you will see yourself & here you will leap & frolic..."

"Sorry, dad, this train don't go in reverse."

9. Where was she? *Deshabillé?* Breath burning on nape. 3 undone buttons going on 4. Him squeezing her clavicles like an accordion, soothing their smooth roundness—"*pelle morbida*."

"All here is holy & virile & pungent & hopeless & unforgettable & prophetic..."

"Shut UP Karol! I know you see the vagina as nothing more than some kind of allegorical coin purse."

9a. Did he also know—the pond, the leap, the contemplation—that she was a member of Venezia's rare *ichthyfauna?* Moonlit calli nymph? That scales (like shingles & scandals) are overlapping bony discs developed from under the skin? That she was convergence of fish & femme, soul & muck? That her caviar birth had left her soulless & thus free of the Great Fisherman of the Sky's net? That at times she wore shells prudently to cover her nipples? That she knew how to be incognito, underground, "be missing," as Raymond Chandler once put it.

10. Did he know that she had once been "volunteered" for

secret U.S. Defense Department Acquatic Mobility Development Projects? Of course he knew. Hadn't he blessed the secret P2-CIA millions of dollars funneled into Poland? Hadn't he condoned the machinations of Opus Dei & the interfacing of CIA, mafia & military regimes? They had, by the late 70s, already successfully mounted nuclear warhead missile launchers onto the dorsal vertebrae of the *delphinidae*, or common dolphin. For a handsome advance they had neonomian plans to mount much lighter anti-sub arms on her shoulder blades until...

11. Did he know that her seductive songs could rival Peggy Lee & could render man "oblivious of this earth," to quote Homer?

But he dreamt on in the linger of his bold stooping genuflection where she caressed his receding hairline, finding the remaining hairs a handhold. He dreamt that she held these last strands as reins. His nose wandering up the inner portion of her tibia, up into her *nectareous entre-jambes* where he hoped this would distract her from broaching, in her charming canine Latin, the subject of the encroaching scandals.

"Are the tellers of the Vatican Bank considered spiritual intermediaries. & what could they tell, Your Holy *Banchiere?*"

"Dead?"

"*Tu Rigolle!*"

"No joke! Wouldn't you rather be absolved of some sins you haven't even committed yet?" (Each attempted probe—"Sindona...Cody...P2...Marcinkus"—into the scandals was met by a strategic nudge of his nose into her exquisite *pinnacula,* her delightful butterfly wings, wink, wink. "*Omerta!*" He demanded her silence.)

"You jivin' me? Are you what you imagine yourself to be? What you've read you're supposed to be? Or what others need to make of you?"

"Wouldn't you like it if I made of you a little *internuncio,* a legate with a little influence in your own bower of exotic flora?"

A recent issue of a Milano Anarchist paper had summed up the emerging corruption scandal with a cartoon. The cartoon detailed the evolution of the cross from its early X-shape to its T-shape to Greek fish-hooked **T** to combination of *T* & **X**-shape as an ✥, then on to its modern day cross shape & from there evolving into bound fasces, swastika, **$** sign & Swiss Franc symbol.

Had he seen it? Huh? But he was absorbed. Absorbing. Regenerating missing maternal memories. Lust & lost. & he sank his face into her *petto exquisito* & licked the nipples & all the bitter blush his tongue found there.

She could show him. She had the clipping with her. So what DID he know? & did knowing really matter when a genius or a fool could be knocked off equally as easily with the .38 special that she'd packed with her deadly sense of self-restraint?

SIX

R.E.M. R.E.M. Stink of potassium nitrate, charcoal & sulfur. Deep profound sleep. Chinese New Year. A gun. John Paul I. Phencyclidine Hallucination. The bitter blush that had tendered his langue had indeed been hi-grade angel dust.

"Deadly sense of self restraint..." The phrase catapulted the dream, luminous ball, out the library window & through dark space, spinning with a kaleidoscope of changing imagery slipping along its surface. (Like Roger Corman's vision of an acid trip.) Flashes of the *corrida;* sweeping reds, galloping browns, jets of chrome flashes, Amoretto posters, pink sands, arena mandela, torreadors in sandals, audience of gondoliers dressed in black. POPO TORO! the gate swung open. The gondoliers roared. Then POW! KAZOOM! IMPACT!

The sphere slams through a ceiling of glass onto a steel bed. Splinters of glass flicker down like asbestos flakes in slo-mo.

In the aftershock the Pope realizes that he was that hurtling globe. That she was its catapult. Her lacy brassiere its sling. His body is now restored to its former glorious state, tied X tight, just right, to the steel bed. 6 inch nails grow like grass beneath his torso. Torches of fire dance on the ends of the copper bedposts. Feelings of deja vu murmur through his veins.

Looking around, he finds he is isolated in what seems to be a large white operating room. Bright light accentuated the starkness of this clinical rotunda.

Bovolo, dressed as a Klaus Barbie doll in a stiff, tailored SS uniform (retrieved for her from the Vatican's secret basement archives), enters. She mounts the bed. Boot heels muff his ears—creamy waxed ankles mere centimeters from his lips. Ankle bones fragile & allusive inside her boot & under her Lido-enhanced *peau*. Her uniform opens & falls the way of her totalitarian charade. Panties ever diaphonously pink. The boots slip off with difficulty, with suction & with all the ecstatic excess of politics made aesthetic, horror made sexy.

The most accelerated part of the dream: The change of situation & space is magical. DISNEY-LIKE: A ROLLER COASTER RIDE. G-force thrust accompanied by the rustle of orgasm / hammered nails / drilled button holes.

The Pope shifts frantically upon the points of steel, & unconsciously maneuvers a pillow between his legs. The bed springs chime & hum Krishna. Of virile submission. Of Vishnu. Of Wishnik—OMOMOMOM. Like a restless opium *rêve* that traverses Super-ego & Subconscious in a single R.E.M.—OMOMOM.

& all the Pope remembers is that she didn't open another button, but instead, opened the butt of her .38 Special, from which she pulled 2 large planks of wood, a hammer & 3 nails. (A drunken holographer's seamless illusion.)

The handle of the hammer has a mysterious phallic quality. Torque, leverage, diameter. OMOMOMOM.

After the D.I.Y. Crucifixion, she places an electric "Lenny Bruce" chair to the left of the bed with a thundering crash & plugs it in. The Pope stares, fascinated, like a Mexican watching the solar eclipse, as objects continue to emerge from the gun butt like elephants from a tube of toothpaste.

A machine gun & blindfold. Then a rope, a long rope, with

which she makes a hangman's noose & hangs from a white cross-beam directly overhead. Then a bottle of acid, which dripped caustically upon his quivering testicles. OMOMOM! Then a guillotine. A clove of garlic, which she forces into his mouth. & 2 radishes, up his nostrils.

The treasures are still not finished. A huge syringe, a bottle of Chianti, a glass & a pair of pink rubber gloves which she immediately slips on. She punctures a cork with a needle & fills a syringe with 1/2 litre of vino, pours herself a glass & sits next to His Holiness.

"I like wine, don't you?" A hearty sip. The Pope is silent. Beyond language, beyond testicular proclamation. The radishes & garlic make his eyes tear. He struggles for breath as his heart pounds its chuckmeat rhythms. Bovolo Barbie drinks her glass & examines the objects that the gun has filled the room with.

"Very contemp, don't you think?" She mimmicks the enthusiasm of a collector. OMOMOM. He pounds his pillow.

"This is West of EDEN, baldy," she whispers in his ear. The word EDEN punctuates his gyrations, which punish, then puncture...breaking the pillow open.

Bovolo peers into the pistol with 1 eye closed. Cherubic wonder fills her visage. Saint-esque? She pulls a rose from its barrel. Holds it close to her eye, trying to photo-memorize its delicate perfection. She looks from rose to ankle & back again. "Do you prefer my ankles or the rose?"

OMOMOMOM. Bovolo places the rose on his chest & with her lipstick draws a ♥ around the flower. White tufts of chest pate add definition to the fragility of the rose.

She stares at the floral-heart configuration in its chest nest, her face takes on a despondent pout. She turns away, fumbles with the gun, says "MONEY'S NO OBJECT, *MON CHERI!*"

Silence. White silence. Suddenly she yells—or something foreign inside her yells: "PLAY LOCK CASTRATE ENGRAVE! PLAY LOCK CASTRATE ENGRAVE!" Like *Notre Belle Dame* echoing heavy bronze. Over & over & over.

And in the cacaphony of bells & voices, he sees a flash, a synaptical spark or, better yet, a gleam of syringe, *vino rosso* entering a vein with fierce medicinal pressure. PUNCTURE RUSH CONFUSION.

The vino takes immediate effect. Things spin. Room goes black. Only the bedpost torches lap at the dark. The radishes have popped from nostrils to farflung corners. The clove of garlic is now fixed in the pucker of his Holy Father *culus*. Bovolo stands naked, om, naked, om, naked at the foot of the bed. Her skin looks terrific. Bronze. Om. Biccioni. Om. Breathing *pelle*. Om. Shimmering scales forged to her *pelle morbide*. Om. The clean stitch seam. Om. Confluence of fish & femme. Om. *Femme & accione*. Blur & whirl. She turns him over, points the revolver at the rose on his chest. Both hands steady her aim.

He sees it happening from 2 or 3 perspectives. (Eye of God.) Time is a bead of protoplasm suspended in a jar of oil. The sound is fantastic inside his head full of sleep. Loud like a sliding mountain. Loud like electrified sky. Like silver bullet entering chamber. Like her hot breath, the trigger cocking, the hammer smashing forward, striking the pointed cylinder of lead (hardened with antimony—antithesis of matrimony.)

BANG!!!

Its metallic path—at 3,000 feet per second—is etched with light, a light leading to his heart. Light & bullet push through petals, skin, bone, muscle, fluids, heart, fluids, muscle, bone, skin, & then exits via his back, terminating its flight with tinny percussion into the steel bed.

Singed petals follow into the jet stream & enter his corpus like pollen, to season his heart. Sowing the soul with seeds of natural history. The body is completely relaxed. Dying. White Oh glory... Oh Glory Be White.

OMOM. OMMmmzzzzzzzz.

The dream "signals" her discreet departure. Now only the electric chair remains, its riveted legs like a contemporary sculpture of a

Minotaur. The silence unbearable. The Pope begins to writhe on the nails... Lost autonomy of the fleeting moment. Unsure skin of a fallen apple.

Blurred eyes open...close...the electric chair seems to be sinking in a vat of petroleum jelly. & then he sees it is not an electric chair but his throne. He's sitting on its velvet platform to the left of the bed. His real bed. He wipes his eyes. Senses his groin. The wet. Vatican silence fills the room.

He gathers the loose down scattered on the floor. He puts a pillow feather in his mouth & drinks a glass of water to wash it down—digested evidence, nocturnal host. The rest of the plumage flickers briefly—a magnesium flash of a dream—in the fireplace.

He sits back on his throne & examines this midnight still-life that whispers of lost lust. He tries to engage the puzzle of elements in his bedroom to jolt his memory. But it is the rose that repeats itself most often & he cannot get far. Only the rose, a very special .38 & a woman with fish scale sequins...

"Blood of Flowers," he whispers, staring at the crumple of soiled sheets hanging from his bed. They tell of an invisible voyage, of promised abandon & delivered release.

"Blood of Flowers," he whispers a 2nd time & lifts himself slightly, prying a notebook from under the velvet cushion. He begins to write. To write a poem. A poem that he figures arises straight from his subconscious. A poem believable only because of its mystery.

EPILOGUE

The Pope manipulates the brass stays of his *Opus Dei Corset.*

The film captures Venice in Winter. The Pope watches from his bed. He likes his bed, the same one the Dead Pope had slept in.

Storms inundate the piazzas with trill upon trill of dark water, & the Pope no longer feels odd sleeping in the same sheets that covered the Dead Pope the night he became The Pope Who Could Not Swim In His Own Vomit to those *uomini di fiducia,* those trusted prelates & backbiting Bishops emboldened by the attitudes of their Pope.

The music was Scarlatti. & too perfect for bankrupt Venice, desolate but still splendid. Its *edificios* up on wooden piles, driven into muck, sink 1/4" per year.

A pity. A tragedy. But a tragedy not nearly as fraught with anxiety as her irascible disappearance. Why? Where? Well, that depended on how much of her was truly ichthyo & how much was virago.

He rang the bell from his 3rd floor bedroom, & asked Sister Vincenza to light another cone of gunpowder-based incense (See *GG-1 Series of Model Poses*) in an old chalice.

The corset had been a gift of gratitude from the Opus Dei Sect. Gratitude because the Pope had prayed at the tomb of its founder. Gratitude because this lent legitimacy & momentum to their bleed & flog cult of hyper-wealthy ultra-crats & their agenda of tidy jackboot trade despotism.

The horsehair corset is lined with 100 inward-pointing prongs. The prongs stimulate the torso, invigorate 7 layers of flesh. Draw blood. Warm blood. The way her fingernails insinuated their intoxicating configurations into him.

Bovolo: Could she really be a siren with scales? Enchantress of the fluid realm with a 4-octave range? & rashes burst upon her skin like a blaze of blossoms. Science advisors & theologians were allied in their contempt for such fanciful speculation, because sirens, or the belief in sirens, repudiates the very bases of both science & Christianity. Yet, the more experts renunciated the more faith made fetishistic certitude out of doubt.

Unscrupulous siren, fishy femme fatale, she hints at a netherworld where a humanoid might breathe, in part, through her skin by the exchange of O_2 & CO_2 between surrounding water & numerous blood vessels near her skin's surface.

& she will be safe (if indeed, she's not just a ruse), he reads, he hopes, he is perturbed by doubt. Her blood temperature will adjust to prevailing weather conditions. Her blood is cold. He knows that. She is cold-blooded.

The Pope is proud. For charisma supercedes information, which supercedes benevolence. & proud he should be for he is his own man. Or, at the very least, a man of his own chosen vice & virtue.

Pinstriped men wrote checks in mid-genuflection. Long queues of pointmen prelates, dingy diplomats, CEOs, generals, press pundits, hoodlum accountants & pop stars waited to kiss his red Fisherman's shoes.

& they thanked him. & they showered him with adulation. & they heaved reprieveful sighs of relief. Because the Pope knew money & how it could be used to consolidate power, & that a state within a state is like vice inside virtue.

The Pope had already decreed: 1. that when a man looks at his wife he commits adultery of the heart; 2. that Catholics who remarry can only receive Holy Communion if they take a vow of celibacy; 3. that oral contraception is a sin even while the Vatican profits from investments in the *Istituto Farmacologico Sereno,* maker of Luteolas, a popular oral contraceptive; 4. the reestablishment of *Humane Vitae* which enforced Papal Authority by denying the notion that the Church was somehow beholden to earthly realities.

In 1988, 10 years after the death of John Paul I, the Pope issued a Papal Bull ([bull—L. *bulla,* knob, boss] 1. a papal edict or official document from the Pope)], stating that Zen & Yoga could "degenerate into a cult of the body," debasing Christian prayer. He said Christian prayer is a "personal & profound dialogue between man & god." As opposed to "some physical exercises which can create a kind of rut, imprisoning the person praying in a spiritual privatism."

In the morning, as on other mornings, after the Venice film, the gunpowder incense & the uncapping of the bottle of perfume (the kind she liked to wear), the heavy regal blankets quilted with gold thread seemed nailed to the floor. As if holding a night of rain. His horsehair C-cup Opus Dei Corset stood in a corner beyond his nightstand, not so much contemptuously as longingly.

& now it is 6 a.m. & he must begin to act with *vigilanti cura.* The odd "pearls of unreason," the effluvia of his misshapen desire have again emerged from the snap-thrust of his groin & have again soiled his sheets. & he knows there are ways to keep the sisters mum. He will emphasize the saintliness of silence in the face of all doubt & toil.

At 7 a.m. he will receive his breakfast & freshly ironed white cassock. They will deliver a vase of fresh-cut flowers & the day's mail. They will change his sheets. Sister Vincenza will administer his shots & then they will burn the soiled sheets without question. For the greater glory of God. & he will offer them quality confessions in the bower of the garden.

He knows there will be no trace. He knows fire purifies. & he knows that is why witches burned. & he knows how well the Vatican's investment plans are doing. But he does not know where Bovolo has retreated to. Or whether she will be back again, with her face that held pain like a glass holds brandy. Wearing her pink bellbottoms & head phones. Listening to Prince.

& he knows the plume of smoke arising from the stack will be grey. He picks up the phone & knows that the assembled in St. Peter's Square will see in it what they will. Stability. Pensions. Profit sharing. He will speak directly to Bishop Marcinkus, "God's Banker" & board member of Bahamian banks. & Marcinkus will agree. It's in his best interest to agree. Yes, the Pope's Bovolo knows too much. "Venezia...P2...Eye of God (Vatican secret service originally est. to hunt & destroy "modernists," est. by the chief spy under Mussolini)...snuff...*sasso in boca.*" Yes, Marcinkus agrees the rock in her mouth will fit & look semi-precious when wet. & this will become her. & this will serve as stark & stylish warning to the others. Marcinkus chuckles when the Pope does. The Pope knows she will thusly talk no more. *Si! Si!*

"*Buono notte. A domani. Se Dio vuole.*" & Marcinkus chuckled because the Pope had chuckled. Marcinkus knew what the Pope knew—that these were the last words the Dead Pope heard. More chuckles. "Good night. Til tomorrow. If God wishes." & the Pope knows, as Marcinkus knows, that ALL is holy & virile & hopeless & unforgettable & prophetic. Fin. ▼

MORE AUTONOMEDIA / SEMIOTEXT(E) TITLES